THE POLITICS OF HOPE

Trevor Blackwell has taught extensively in adult education and has worked as a Research Associate at the Centre for Contemporary Cultural Studies where he was co-author of *Paper Voices* (1975), a study of the post-war popular press. Jeremy Seabrook was a teacher and social worker before he became a freelance writer in 1977. He is the author of a number of books, including *Life and Labour in a Bombay Slum* (1987). He has also co-written plays for the theatre, television and radio, and he contributes regularly to the *Guardian*.

Trevor Blackwell and Jeremy Seabrook teach at the Working Men's College. Their previous book *A World Still To Win: The Reconstruction of the Post War Working Class* (Faber, 1985), was described by the *Guardian* as 'One of the most important books on working-class politics . . . in the last 30 years.'

by the same authors

A World Still to Win
*The Reconstruction of
the Post-War Working Class*

The Politics of Hope

BRITAIN AT THE END OF THE TWENTIETH CENTURY

Trevor Blackwell
and Jeremy Seabrook

faber and faber

LONDON · BOSTON

First published in 1988
by Faber and Faber Limited
3 Queen Square London WC1N 3AU

Photoset by Parker Typesetting Service Leicester
Printed in Great Britain by
Cox & Wyman Reading Berks

British Library Cataloguing in Publication Data

Blackwell, Trevor
The politics of hope.
1. Great Britain. Social conditions
I. Title II. Seabrook, Jeremy,
941.085'8
ISBN 0-571-15220-1

The Pharisees also with the Sadducees came, and tempting desired him that he would show them a sign from heaven.

He answered and said unto them, When it is evening, ye say, It will be fair weather: for the sky is red.

And in the morning, It will be foul weather to day: for the sky is red and lowring. O ye hypocrites, ye can discern the face of the sky; but can ye not discern the signs of the times?

Matthew 16, i–iii.

CONTENTS

PREFACE

This book is about the decay of one of the great sustaining myths of our era – the hope and promise of socialism. We have not written it as an exercise in theory, but we have chosen to tell how the exhaustion of the socialist story has been bound up with our own lives and feelings. It is only now that the waning of socialism is further advanced that we can see it for what it has been – a vital and nourishing faith.

We have called upon our own experience, not because our lives have any exceptional significance, but because they share with the lives of our generation a common impress of the historical moment through which we have passed. What is important is not so much that we have lived through these times as that they have lived through us: we bear their scars, but we also bear witness to those scarrings.

This is not a book about disillusionment. It may chart the decline of faith in one incarnation of the politics of hope, but it also shows how social hope does not die in the world, but, rather, struggles to find new and more adequate manifestations. The forms of life-giving myth perish and pass away, but their essence is carried forward in new hopeful stories (often themselves very old ones indeed) which can inspire a new generation. While Labourism languishes, and Communism is corrupted, the hopes of Socialism are passing into the deep green philosophy which makes the most radical promise of a sustainable and wholesome life for all on earth.

ACKNOWLEDGEMENTS

We would like to thank the following people who have discussed with us some of the themes of this book: Victor Anderson, Caroline Hutchison, Bob Clark, Cindy Harris, Val Remy, Aine Walsh, Stephanie Smolenski, Terry Woods, David Brownridge, Ivan and Wisia Ruff, Janet Ashworth, Barry Davis, Derek Hooper, Michael O'Neill, Jane and Michael Bradbury and Winin Pereira.

Our thanks are offered again to all our students at the Working Men's College, who continue to explore these issues with us week by week.

We would also like to thank the editors of the *Guardian* and *New Society* for permission to publish extracts from material which first appeared there.

PART ONE
Feelings

I

Rage, helplessness, a sense of redundancy; a feeling of being in exile, of disappointment and dividedness; loathing, contempt and fear, a dread of being suffocated; a disabling self-doubt.

These are our feelings, living in Britain in the late 1980s. How different they are from anything we anticipated, as we were growing up in that changed world which our parents had won for us after 1945. Our future at that time appeared expansive and filled with hope, not only personal hope, but also a belief that the society in which we were to take our place was getting better, morally as well as materially. Modest though the lives of our families might have been, we felt they were nevertheless bequeathing to us something of great worth: a vision of a better world that was in the process of being realized. They gave us to understand that this involved a decisive break with the punishing and destructive aspects of the life they had known; and we believed them. They were even slightly envious of us, for they felt that they might not live to see the furthest consequences of the changes they had helped to enact. 'There never were such times', they said, not without some self-satisfaction, as each new possibility appeared in their lives – their children starting off married life with new furniture, being able to eat frozen peas in December, being able to imagine work outside of the mill or the factory. The world was opening up to those who had been so pinched and cramped in the cold little houses in towns where everything that mattered was within walking distance, and the high cloudy moors marked the beginnings of an unfamiliar outside world, a world into which exploratory outings could be made only on special days and with adequate provisions.

If our harsh and violent feelings were only the expected, traditional disappointments that come with middle age, if they were the result of having to shed heroic illusions, a reluctant acknowledgement of the limits that define all our lives, they would still be hard to bear. They would not, though, weigh us down as they do now, in a degraded social landscape, where the withering of public hope further blights the unsatisfied yearnings of individuals. We are well aware of what getting older is about. Indeed, the examples of fortitude and endurance in the people with whom we grew up were part of our true education; and there is plenty to complain about in that. We are well able to detach our feelings about what cannot be remedied in this life from the collapse of a belief that together we would be able to achieve what we never could alone – a good life.

Our parents believed, indeed vowed, that there would be no going back. There would be no return to the all too familiar indifference towards the old suffering, towards the pain of individuals who existed as such only in so far as they replaced hands that faltered at the loom, or raised another generation and kept them in line to serve in their turn. This vow was made in earnest and on our behalf by those who nurtured us and fought for us; we were to be the living evidence that it had been kept.

So it came about that our every achievement was celebrated as an allegory of the new dispensation – being able to do joined-up writing before starting school, being able to name things that had been known only in the local and half-shaming dialect (knowing, for instance, that titty-bottles were really white campion, and that the much-consulted 'doctor's book' was really a medical encyclopedia), the almost accentless voice with which we recited poetry to astonished aunts and uncles; these attainments easily merged with more tangible social benefits, the round and brindled spectacle frames, the leg-irons, the free orange juice, the malt and the rose-hip syrup which eliminated the avoidable sicknesses of childhood.

We absorbed a powerful sense of changed expectations which it would somehow fall to us to fulfil. It could scarcely have occurred to us that we would ever be called upon to defend those changes, though had we listened more carefully to our parents' stories from a mythical period called *pre-war*, we might have heard hidden in their gratitude a warning that what has been given can also be taken away. Just as their vow was sworn on no sacred book, but on the flesh and blood of those they loved, so any resolve we made to keep faith was a subject of no solemn ceremony: we never dreamed it would ever be put to the test. It all seemed beyond dispute.

Exactly what our parents expected in return for these gifts was never made explicit. What they wanted from us turned out to be ambiguous and contradictory. It soon became clear that we were required to change without becoming different. Most of what we knew from home would not pass in the outside world into which we were sent as both champions and vindicators. For one thing, we had to become bilingual, with all the pride and shame which that involved. And then, many of the material things that originated at home were in some mysterious way unworthy, not good enough because they were different, and therefore obscurely inferior. We remember throwing away the home-made tomato sandwiches on the school outing because they weren't dainty enough, the bread had been too crudely cut; a satchel was 'lost' over the cemetery wall, even though made of best leather which an uncle had stolen from his workplace, because it was too unwieldy and roughly-made in comparison to the smooth, shiny artefacts which the other pupils wore on their backs. We could never escape a feeling that there was something wrong with our clothes, even though the school uniform had been bought at the approved school supplier at inordinate expense. When we tentatively employed the homely wisdom of family sayings – 'What can't be cured must be endured', or 'There's nothing done without trouble except letting the fire out', or 'It's a sign of a hard winter when the hay starts running after the horse' – they would come back sharply underlined in red with 'cliché' written in the margin. This unacceptability became more pervasive and more wounding as we progressed up the school: it came as a great shock when the teacher took out a copy of the paper which was delivered every day at home to illustrate the deficiencies of popular taste. We squirmed with embarrassment when our mother or grandmother insisted on visiting our school in response to an invitation to discuss our progress. How could they understand the answers the teacher might have given, when they weren't even sure what questions to ask, beyond a timid 'And how's he getting on then?' Removing the ornamental pin from their best hats afterwards, they said what a nice man the history teacher was, and what a good report he had given us. We suspected, however, that we knew the real meaning of his kindness: he had patronized them with the greatest urbanity because he realized they hadn't the foggiest idea of what he was talking about. We were uncertain whether to be flattered or insulted by the collusive messages we felt he was transmitting to us through their innocence.

These ambiguities made us all the more determined to uphold the superior values of the world from which we came – the decencies, the respect for hard work, the honesty, the generosity, the morality of doing as you would be done by, the resolute refusal to be impressed by station or status, and the levelling humour that celebrated our common condition. These things had taken root in us, they were part of our substance; so much so that we didn't need to articulate them to ourselves, although, as we ascended into higher education, we found ourselves ever more frequently describing them to others. These values were certainly not ubiquitous in the settings through which we lived – we all knew families who were shiftless, whose behaviour was a source of much inexhaustible scandalized gossip, or who were up the pub every night spending what ought to have gone into the bellies of their children – but they were present in the places that really mattered. They pervaded our homes and the homes of our friends. All the adults we knew were at work, and the only people you saw during the daytime were old people and mothers, who were the only social groups who didn't have to justify being seen in public during working hours. The same philosophy of life was exemplified in the modest entertainment at chapel socials, the noisy enjoyment of beetle drives, and the hilarity over potato pie suppers to which everyone contributed; and even in the corner pubs they were always collecting for a wreath for somebody who had died. Even though these homely values were not to be found in the grammar school or, for the most part, on radio or, later, on television, and certainly not in the newspapers, this didn't seem to be important. We knew that most people didn't go to grammar school anyway, and we didn't expect their voices to be heard on radio or TV except as comic caricatures. We felt that we not only had right on our side, but also the numbers to back it up: if it came to a showdown – whatever that might mean – we knew we wouldn't be the losers. We felt that our journey into the grammar-school world was rendered less perilous because in the event of failure, there remained an alternative, welcoming and always available. If we stumbled in our progress, they always said to us 'Never mind. You can only do your best.' And there remained the example of the young man who had been up in court for, of all the humiliating and disgraceful things, stealing women's underclothes from washing lines and dressing up in them, and whose mother defiantly told the neighbours 'He's still my son, and this is where he belongs'; and we felt, perhaps over-optimistically, that our own failures would be far less shaming than this.

If our initial reaction to grammar school was one of secret terror at its power and arrogance, we kept it from our anxious parents. By the time we got to the sixth form, we had gained enough self-confidence to mock its complacency and sense of its own dignity. We could then see ourselves as explorers, an advance party, raiders in another culture, potentially hostile, which we would exploit for ends other than those for which access to it had been granted.

For those of us brought up within the chapel community, there was danger and security in our oscillation between the two worlds. The grammar school was dangerous because it was both posh and godless; our security was that we still shared the strength of a working-class culture, and that we felt morally superior because we were 'saved'. Our Sunday-school teachers told us that what we needed to learn at school was to speak to the world in its own terms. There had been delivered to us a truth that was precious and imperishable. It was our duty to take this with us wherever we went. In this endeavour we must be as wise as serpents, though as harmless as doves.

For those of us with a background in the trade unions, it was a question of seizing the knowledge that would enable us to stand up to the owners and bosses and managers, not to shuffle and cough in their presence, but to look them fearlessly in the eye, and to manipulate words against them, just as they had always done against us. We were in fact the inheritors of a people only recently literate, and we carried with us the reverence for words of the newly lettered. Above all, we believed in words and their power to dominate circumstance. After all, had not our ability to use words transformed our own situation? We imagined that we would filch words of power from those who had been long set over us. Our mastery of language would not only take away from the people we loved their sense of subordination, but at the same time would reduce the authority of those who had dominated them, and into whose culture, it seemed, we were now being initiated.

It wasn't as clear-cut as that, especially in the beginning. There were always contradictions and tensions, but for a long time these remained in balance, and therefore tolerable. Our personal progress – even spectacular advancement – seemed to go hand in hand with a more general social betterment, and for as long as this continued, the contradictions remained muted; a matter of *personal* anxiety and *self*-questioning. Our rewards and achievements, which seemed to us surprisingly effortless, were a confirmation of what we knew, which was the worth of our own people. Thus the praise we received had its material counterpart in the improved circumstances of our parents' lives. As they were able to convert the little back bedroom into an inside toilet and bathroom, as the gleaming cream refrigerator replaced the metal safe in which food had too often gone bad, as the scrubbed deal table was replaced by a contemporary dining-room suite, this seemed to indicate that they, like us, were getting something closer to what they deserved. It began to seem as if for the first time the cycle of work, want and war was being broken. What more fitting celebration could there be than to see their children ascending into social spheres to which they had formerly raised their eyes only in reverential wonder or envious rancour?

Their lives had never been more secure; and this meant that they could afford to allow us to set off on our journeys of exploration. We were no longer economically needed at home; whether we ate meat or not on Sunday did not depend on us handing over a weekly wage-packet. Our privileged trajectory was one of the first luxuries they permitted themselves. All the agonizing about whether we should stay on at school – should we, dare we? – was histrionics. The decision had already been settled, not by the portentous advice of form masters or career advisers, but by the fact that we were not required to look after our family in those basic material ways which had been expected of all previous generations. After all, they were safely in work (as though work had become some kind of permanent fortification against destitution), and the welfare state was in place, which reassured us that if our grandmother fell down in the street, the ambulance would be there within minutes, and that our parents would be relieved of any worry about paying the rent when they got older by the certainty that the old-age pension would replace the weekly wage. So it was safe for us to leave. Henceforth, it seemed the things that would continue to attach us to them would be the freely renewed dependencies of human need rather than the brutal exigencies of economic necessity.

The affirming evidence that we had reached the right decision was soon all about us. We would boldly go and seek our fortune by way of higher education, even though deep changes in the social and economic structure of Britain had already sought it for us. Our liberation was part of wider liberating influences that continued to lift up our people and at the same time to transform society, irradiating it with the values of which we thought we were the bearers and custodians. At that time, all the changes we had lived through still looked benign. We and those like us (and who didn't want to be like us?) were in the ascendant. Simultaneously, figures of power and authority, those same people who had sat on the Board of Guardians and denied our parents the half-crown that would have enabled them to go to the High School, who had given them food vouchers during the Depression, so that they wouldn't spend their public assistance money on cigarettes and frivolities, were, it seemed, being dethroned from their high position. This iconoclasm was strengthened by the irreverent and mocking humour which was unmistakably ours, and which was bursting for the first time into the mass media, where we heard our own accents make fun of those who still considered themselves to be our elders and betters. Bishops, Members of Parliament, the royal family, colonels in their country estates, retired colonial administrators, débutantes, Lady Bountifuls and the purveyors of charity to the poor all became instant figures of fun. It seemed the rich had had their day. With what joy we discovered that we were not only on the right side, but also fashionable. Our success and our concerns were reflected in the growth of the caring agencies of the State, social work, education, the new universities, youth and community work. If caring came to be spoken of for the first time as a profession, rather than as an attribute of that daily life we had witnessed as children, we regarded this as an extension rather than as an expropriation. It seemed that the convictions that had been so deeply imprinted upon us were gaining wider and more intense social expression. Social progress seemed assured: it was all part of a resistless forward movement that was positive, necessary and deeply desirable. If this was not yet *our* society, at least we were able to recognize in it our own critical sensibilities, as well as a more distant reflection of the people from whom we had inherited them. Society everywhere offered us back images of ourselves, all vital and flattering. The working class was being celebrated as never before. We celebrated the moment, and felt ourselves celebrated by it.

2

These social transformations seemed to be in sympathy with deeper personal needs.

Homosexuality was denied absolutely in the working-class community, and assumed to be something that those who had more money than was good for them got up to. In any case, it was a subject of abhorrence and contempt. Homosexuality – as it was then universally designated – was associated with the Sunday papers: stories of detectives keeping watch for seven nights in succession in a public lavatory in Mablethorpe, of unspeakable things that men did together, which were referred to as acts of gross indecency. We were warned in ways so oblique as to be

incomprehensible to avoid men who might attempt to do things to
you in the pictures, try to interfere with you. If we inquired what
this meant, the response was likely to be 'Never you mind. Just
keep away from it.' Dismissed scoutmasters and defrocked vicars
occasionally figured in hushed conversations, full of significant
silences. 'Please God, may it never happen to anybody belonging
to us', Auntie May would sigh, after reading some more than
usually shocking revelation in her copy of the *News of the World*.
We were disturbed by their response to these horrors, for they
provided us with the first intimations that being *different* could
have negative as well as positive charges. Long before we knew
that we were gay, we felt a driving curiosity about these stig-
matized individuals and an obscure implication in their shame. As
time went by, it dawned upon us that this could be part of the
belatedly revealed price which had to be paid for our spectacular
success. It felt like a curse, an affliction; something almost too
dreadful to be acknowledged.

 How were we to deal with this enormity? We went to the library,
perhaps predictably, in the hope that there we might find the
words that would reveal to us who we were, and what we should do
with ourselves. Under the stare of the disapproving librarian, we
took down books with titles like *The Psychology of Sex* and *Sexual
Deviations and their Treatment*. In the chapter labelled 'Homosexuality', we were mildly relieved to learn that it was now
recognized to be a sickness rather than a sin. The homosexual
could be quite easily identified. He (it was never she) often had
artistic inclinations. His condition could be detected from his
physique, which was marked by an absence of facial hair, and a
tendency to accumulate fat around the buttocks. This made us
look sideways at our reflection in shop windows as we walked
down the High Street. From there we might go to the local
museum, among the limited exhibits of which was a Greek frieze
with statues of naked men, with whom we could surreptitiously

compare ourselves – to, it seemed, our extreme disadvantage.

We resisted the knowledge gained from these explorations, because of what we knew it would mean. We would be excluded from that comfort and warmth and love which was our family's most precious gift to us. Far from being the standard-bearers of our class, we would be rudely cast out. This shameful consciousness gnawed at and diminished all our public achievements. It was a contradiction scarcely to be contemplated; so we didn't contemplate it. Part of the prodigious energy that we then directed into learning and studying and succeeding came from this denial and suppression of what we suspected was our real nature. Perhaps if we didn't think about it, it would go away. It didn't. It stared us in the face, loomed out of the precocious triumphs that our formal learning made possible.

Later it seemed that being homosexual was a kind of tribute paid for the journey out of our class. It was a journey into a double exile. It was as though in leaving our class we had also left our gender. We had lost a certain way of being masculine in the world, and all our studies failed to yield us another, no matter how deeply we searched our books.

Although we might have expressed total revulsion from stereotyped working-class maleness, we were in fact less repelled than we cared to admit. It was precisely the absence of such attributes in ourselves which created the need to compensate for an inner emptiness. And what more effective way than to distance ourselves from those models, with whose maleness we felt we had so little in common, but who possessed something essential that we secretly longed for.

Our ambiguity was not totally misplaced. For one thing, there was something desirable in that unreflecting maleness. It offered a way of existing which was quite unselfconscious and uncontaminated by doubt. And then, working-class maleness was always more subtle and adaptable than some contemporary ideological versions of it would suggest. In many areas of experience, the dependence of working-class men on women was almost total: without them, the men shrank and were diminished. This dependence found its more overt acknowledgement in an awkward tenderness at times of illness, in the broken avowal at the funeral of how much she had meant to him. The image of the elderly man wheeling his wife in a clumsy metal chair is no isolated example, doing for her all the things she could no longer manage to do for herself, and discovering that he could wash and clean and feed her, and that what he had always considered women's work could also be part of being a man. The son who stayed at home to look after his mother, openly declaring that he would never get married and that his Mam was his only sweetheart, was not an object of ridicule but a valued member of the community. Men working on the allotments, growing flowers, tending birds, tell another story; men making toys for their children, spending hours on waggons, sledges or wooden dolls, suggest less aggressive concerns.

If it seemed impossible to return to the working class as its homosexual children, perhaps this was partly because we underestimated how accommodating and accepting and open working-class people could be. We knew to what degree they could also be intolerant and dismissive of what was not immediately understandable in terms of their own life experience; and it was this that made us keep silence when the moment came for us to speak. Those positive qualities, which many individual working-class people came to through personal discovery, were never fully developed socially. Indeed, they tended to atrophy for lack of cultural nourishment.

One of the principal reasons for this failure lay in the limited nature of the success of the Labour Movement in 1945. If we are to understand the decay of political hope in contemporary Britain, we need to grasp the real meaning of that famous victory. 1945 has always been depicted as a high point, even as a culmination of

Labour's endeavours, whereas it should have been regarded as the merest beginnings of that process of deepening political awareness that had been accelerated by the war years. Thus, the setting up of the welfare state was seen as the triumphant embodiment of all that Labour believed in and had worked for. It is, of course, true that it gave expression to the best instincts of a class bred in adversity, but its effects were far more ambiguous. For the ways in which the welfare state operated involved a seizure of those generous impulses, and a locking of them into administrative structures that expropriated and institutionalized them. What ought to have remained as living and familiar responses to each other's needs and woes became frozen in the caring machinery of the State. We should not therefore be surprised when those agencies put in place to humanize a cruel social system are perceived by the people as remote and alien and acting against their interests.

Whilst it may be idle to speculate on the might-have-beens of political history, it is nevertheless fruitful to retrieve those living possibilities that have been suppressed and inhumed in the garden of rest of licensed nostalgias. A more creative development of the rudimentary consciousness of 1945 than that which capitalism has permitted would without doubt have meant that we would now be living in a very different society, a society far better equipped to tackle the global problems of our age. The loss is incalculable, which may be why it fails to appear in any capitalist balance-sheet, however rigorously audited it may be. For what has been bypassed is the beginnings of a real tolerance of human diversities, as opposed to the intolerance concealed beneath the showy options of free markets: the markets may be free, but what of the people who must remain in bondage to them?

3

It was the stunting of the capacity of any growth other than economic which made the liberal moment of the 1960s appear to be so much at odds with popular sentiment. Even so, there were strong traces of working-class tolerance (people said 'Live and let live', 'There's good and bad in all of us', 'It takes all sorts', 'I take people as I find them', 'It wouldn't do for us all to be the same'), and it almost looked as if it might some day be possible to reconcile being gay and working-class. Such feelings were perhaps as much based on our future hopes as on the existing reality; but it remains true that our lives then represented an unfolding, an opening up, an expansiveness, which made this country a more decent and humane place than it had ever been. If on political marches and demonstrations the gay liberation contingent drew sidelong and less than enthusiastic glances from trade unionists, at least they didn't reject our support in a cause which we appeared to share. The common struggle offered a hope of eventual reconciliation; one day, it seemed, we would be able to go home again.

Throughout the 1960s we had been aware of no oppressive burden of labour which would cramp our search for a fuller life. Work could be taken up and set down at will. Anybody could teach, and there was always casual work available for the asking. The idea of embarking single-mindedly upon a career seemed strange, and indeed, somewhat beneath us. We had more important things to do. We had ourselves and other territories to discover; and if these explorations could be of benefit to others, so much the better. We did not disdain some occasional political and community work, the latter almost invariably in places where we were not resident; adult education claimed our interest for a time; we gave ourselves up totally, if briefly, to experiments in communal living. In so far as we thought about the Labour Party at all, it seemed to us obviously redundant, hopelessly outgrown by a generation scarcely aware of its own debt to Labour's earlier achievements.

How easy it had all been! No longer constrained and bounded by material want, there was a curious absence of struggle in our triumphal progress through the world. Each year brought a more splendid and exotic harvest. We got up at four o'clock in the morning to catch the milk train at the beginning of our first trip to the continent, a place tainted for our parents as a site of war. We went to parties where we met people who had actually written books which we went to look at later on the library shelves. We were welcomed into the spacious interiors of those who were successful and who had good taste as well – so unlike those who had been eager to show off their overblown and stifling drawing rooms in the provincial home town. Though outwardly we took it all as a matter of course, we hugged ourselves in secret and said 'This is something our parents would never have been able to do in a million years.'

It was possible to wander in and out of the professions, as though these were merely french windows on the stage set of our lives. All doors swung effortlessly open, as though simply waiting for our magic touch. We would go from the role of teacher to that of social worker, from that of community activist to journalist to WEA lecturer. How easy it was to avoid the snare of being trapped in a single occupation; how we despised the incremental progression of those of our peers already calculating their pension entitlements. We pitied them because they, unlike us, had not realized how radically the world had changed. It seemed there were vast areas of our being that escaped the constricting classifications of work. What do you do? we were asked, and we replied, according to our humour, 'I'm doing research' or 'I write' or 'I'm helping to organize against a motorway', or 'I'm just into being', or with some petulance, 'I don't *do* anything.' Alternatively, we claimed to be working on a building site/in a café/on the assembly line, or to be collecting material (for a novel, it was understood). Often, we would say 'Oh I'm into meditation', as though that were sufficient occupation in itself. Some people we knew would be planning to take a Volkswagen to India; and indeed, it took Trevor only six weeks of working at Cadbury's Bournville factory to earn enough money for a one-way ticket to India. 'I never had any intention of coming back. I was going to find a small village and live with the people; or I was going to arrive at a monastery and be recognized as the special person I was. It seemed the obvious – the only – thing to do. This was the climax of the successive escapes of which my life had until then consisted. It had the added advantage that a journey to the East postponed, perhaps indefinitely, any necessity to get a job, to locate myself in a specific place or a particular class in British society. It was an attempt to reject all limitations: class, Englishness, Methodism, British imperialism, Western sensibility in general, even the twentieth century. I was seeking the realm of perfect freedom. Such a fantastic project seemed plausible – was written into the opportunities and the ignorance which characterized our progress through the 1960s.'

We ought to have known; but having had no political education which remotely approached the persuasiveness and penetration of the instruction received from capitalist culture, we rested in the simple certitudes of our parents, which had stopped at 1945, like the clock on some grandiose monument rendered forever obsolete by the war. The better world which had been promised had duly been ushered in, and all we had to do was live in it. If the Age of Aquarius rested somewhat awkwardly upon its 1945 foundations, we never for one moment doubted that the old things had passed away. Our experience was only a little further removed from the conviction of our parents that a once-and-for-all break had been made with the old world of restriction and poverty and insecurity. Our true education – as opposed to the formal, official version, which we had nevertheless managed, by dint of generous grants, to spin out well into our twenties – was about to begin. Our parents had sometimes threatened us with a rude awakening – 'You don't know you're born', 'You've got it all to learn', 'You'll know one day'. These half-envious admonitions were born from their residual knowledge that the world had never worked like this before, that there must be a catch in it somewhere, although nobody quite knew what it was; and from a secret guilt that they didn't deserve the good times they were having, of which our good times were only a more fantastic extension. They were warning themselves as well as us; and quite rightly, because we were the symbols of the changes. All the silences between us, the resentment, the incomprehension (what was glibly designated by the media 'the generation gap'), what we saw as their limited experience, and what they perceived as our ignorant triumphalism, condensed to form a thick fog which shrouded the contours of the social landscape in which we of course all still lived.

These were the true causes of the awkwardnesses in our conversations whenever we went home, of the oblique unasked questions, when they said 'Are you looking after yourself properly?'; 'It doesn't sound much of a job, after all the education you've had'; 'Why do you have to go all that way to be a teacher – don't they need teachers round here?' Apart from that, there seemed to be no need to make any more searching inquiries into what was happening to us, because whatever it was appeared so plainly beneficial to all concerned. Everything seemed to confirm that they had been right to relinquish their control of us so many years before. They were curiously estranged from us as one of the effects of those social changes which had begun with so much celebration in the 1940s, but which had assumed an independent life of their own, and such ambiguous shape also; ambiguous, in the sense that everything was getting better, even though they were troubled by an obscure sense of dislocation, unease and loss.

They could speak to us only in parables. 'They've opened what they call a supermarket. They had that woman with the big bosoms to open it, what's her name . . . Traffic came to a standstill. I didn't go, I don't know what all the fuss is about. Anyway, Florrie Atkinson, she only went in there to have a look round, but she walked out with a tin of red salmon under her pinafore. They stopped her, just when she got outside the door, swore she'd stole it. She said she couldn't remember, she'd been having blackouts. They pinched her. Five pound fine. It was in the paper, her name and everything. Anyway, she ended up putting her head in the gas-oven.' And we would say 'Who's Florrie Atkinson? I don't know her.' 'Yes you do, big woman, lived over the back.' 'I can't remember.'

We brushed such stories aside, perhaps because we were too disturbed by them. We also knew there was something wrong, but at a level which neither they nor we had any language for. In spite of our expensive erudition, we failed to recognize the literary discourse they were employing in their attempt to reach us, traditional though this was. Thus again: 'They buried Mrs Collins last week. Her daughter never turned up. Not for her own mother's funeral. It appears they fell out twenty years ago over some money, a few quid he left. She used to walk past her in the street, her own daughter, and not speak . . . It was the neighbour who found her. She went straight round to fetch the daughter. She didn't want to know. They say blood's thicker than water. Don't you believe it.'

These sombre narratives always irritated us; what were we supposed to say? And then somebody had been found dead in the flats, having lain for a fortnight undetected; no detail was omitted, of the buzzing flies or what the dog, driven mad by hunger, had done. Any interest we might have had in familiar gossip was diminished by the unmistakable sense that these instructive tales were in some way directed at us, and were full of unspoken

reproach and appeals, which they had long since given up any
right to make more overtly. 'How long are you home for this
time?' they asked, or even 'How long are you on leave for?'
because the only precedent they knew for leaving home was the
army. It is futile to speculate upon who was more damaged by
this collusive yet involuntary silence. It was the consequence of a
common loss. Going home reminded us that the freedoms in
which we exulted were the result of wider and deeper
fragmentations, over which neither we nor they had any control
at all. The conversations that we should have had could only be
patterned through the silences.

4

So when did we start to learn? It wasn't quite like that; it was
rather a kind of incredulous waking up, as though we had
sleep-walked for a large part of our lives. Since 1979 a harsher
and clearer light has been cast upon the hopes, the evasions and
fantasies which made up the 1960s, and of which we were both
the bearers and the living incarnation. Through the 1970s, we
had intimations and prefigurings. There was a growing sense of
the unsustainability of how we were living in the world. The
foreshadowings presented themselves at several levels. When
Trevor returned from India in 1970, his passport confiscated
and suffering from a bad case of jaundice, the first thing he
noticed was that the Conservative and Labour Parties seemed to
have changed places. On TV Harold Wilson was talking about
how we must conserve what we had achieved, while Heath was
talking urgently of the need for change and radical transformation. The atmosphere of the miners' strike of 1973/4, with its
suggestion of siege and chaos, reached the point of apocalypse
when the TV sets went off and city streets were plunged into
darkness at curfew time. It was like the war all over again, but

now, we were told, the enemy was within: and the enemy were nothing less than the heroes of the Labour Movement. Wilson's unexpected victory in 1974 gave pause to this momentum. The years 1974–9 were a time of waiting and expectancy: a series of tableaux, while the Labour Party demonstrated, in swiftly shifting scenes, the limits of its possibilities and the exhaustion of its energies. Although it came as a shock, it seemed oddly appropriate that Wilson should resign in mid-term. At the time he was suspected of knowing of some dreadful catastrophe that was just around the corner. And indeed, who is to say that intuitively, as the leader of the Labour Movement who was, above all, identified with the 1960s, he was not aware that a long-deferred moment of truth was about to arrive?

By the late 1970s it seemed incredible that this could be the party that had been the vehicle of the heroic moment of transformation in 1945. It was as though the ghost of the Labour Partry has returned to its old home, and found that everything in it had been used up by others. It came back to govern in a world which it had itself helped to shape, but which had become unrecognizable, and intractable to its control. It was its destiny to show that, far from being able to continue to transform society, it could not even sustain the improvements it had set in train.

At a deeper level, the failures of Labour through the 1970s illuminated the true nature of the regeneration of Britain, and indeed, of the whole Western world, in the post-war period.

The apprehension that something had gone wrong, that a promise had not been fulfilled, was felt by many in ways that never appeared in any overt public and political signals. Even in the 1960s, some had tentatively expressed the suspicion that what came to be known as 'the consumer society' did not represent the true materialization of the people's dreams; although at that time, it was very difficult to say in what way it was either inadequate or deformed. Indeed, there was a taboo on any questioning of 'what the people wanted' which, by a happy coincidence, was what already existed in the world with such showy omnipresence. The faintest hint of scepticism about the shape and direction of material progress as currently being lived was sufficient to have oneself branded killjoy, puritan, snob, elitist. 'Why shouldn't ordinary people [those in whose name so many ignoble endeavours have been unleashed in the world] have what the rich have always taken for granted?' – 'You want to kick the ladder away now that you've made it yourself.' – 'Who are you to say what is good for other people?' – 'If you want to control people's lives, go to Russia.'

This over-reaction was so extreme that it is necessary to probe both its origin and function. What were those brave defenders of the people afraid of? What was the nature of their fierce defensiveness? Was it because any reservations about 'the consumer society' came close to drawing aside the mantle that had been thrown over the true meaning of the reconstruction of 1945?

What had occurred in the 1930s, and in the war that followed, had reduced what we were pleased to think of as the heart of civilization in the world to the site of irrationality, barbarism and ashes. To many it seemed as though something essential about capitalism had been unmasked (though others preferred to see in it revelations of the iniquity of human nature; and who is to say that both were not at least partly right?). Some had glimpsed in that violence and slaughter what always remains one possible form of capitalist necessity. For at times of extreme economic disorder, a system in disarray must project its own threat to human life upon one particular group or class of human beings; in this case, the Jews. The liberal certainties of the West had been shaken. It seemed as if economic forces had emerged from their abstract and recondite operations in the capitalist system, and had been made flesh and blood under the insignia of the swastika and the jackboot. Those who surveyed the ruins of Europe, who saw the people grubbing for survival among the rubble of the cities of Germany, and to whom the task of reconstruction would be entrusted, were dealing with something more than material devastation: there had also been a spiritual collapse. Because it was through the breakdown of the economy that the true nature of capitalism had been revealed, it became of immediate and desperate importance to conceal the enormities that had been laid bare. Accordingly, reconstruction came to mean, above all else, the rehabilitation of those disgraced economic forces. Of course it is true that there was nothing that the people needed more than the material prerequisites for survival; but it was not with that primary objective that the economy was reconstructed. Economic growth and expansion rapidly came to be an embodiment of hopes and energies, spiritual as well as physical, for which they were at best an imperfect, and in certain respects a quite improper, vehicle. They were indeed to become the sponge that was passed over that particular episode in European history. Growth and expansion were to become an expiatory impulse, they were to cancel all previous wrongs; in short, they were to become redemptive, in a way that socialist ideology had sought in vain to be.

Once this act of faith is made, the memory is laved and the burden lifted from the consciousness of the people, and anything and everything that further this process is permissible, indeed required. And then the economy has finally established itself at the heart of all political, social and moral discourse. The performance of the economy becomes the object of the greatest anxiety and solicitude; and only its continuing satisfactory workings can guarantee that the guilt will remain allayed, the responsibility for what happened will go on being dissipated. In this way, memory dissolves under the quicklime of the mass graves that litter the European charnel-house.

The reverence for the economic was rooted in the bones of the victims of the system that was about to be reconstructed. Here is the earth, enriched with human remains, on which the post-war economic miracle took place. Why such 'miracles' should be necessary is passed over in silence. Those who lament – and especially those who would celebrate – the diminishing of political debate into an obsessive concern with which party can make the economy work (or in later jargon, 'perform') better should consider the beginnings of the new dispensation. The role of Labour and of Socialist parties in this work of rebuilding was two-fold. First of all, to provide illusions that the new beginnings actually represented a radical break with the past, the will to create a new society which would articulate the hopes and desires of their own people; and secondly, and more prosaically, to provide a scaffolding of welfare services which would both support and shroud the restoration of the old structures – just as the whole of Europe was later to be covered with perfect replicas, imitations and reproductions of its architectural heritage that had been pounded into dust. The medieval city centre, the old castle, the damaged cathedral, the city hall, the museums were to exhibit no traces of the violence that had obliterated them.

A society built on corpses must not be too surprised if the smell of putrefaction penetrates even the strongest deodorants it can produce, nor if its people develop a fascination with death.

This fascination must be worked out in the world; as indeed it is. The unnecessary death toll throughout the Third World, from malnutrition, curable sickness, infant mortaility, and wars fought with arms inscribed with the names of rich entreprencurs in the industrial world, is structured into the way we live. Our ever-rising standards of material consumption are a species of cannibalism, for we are eating up the very substance of the world's poor. The necessities of the poor are converted, by the need for profit, into items of indifferent daily use by the rich. There is death in the Ethiopian courgettes, the Brazilian mangoes, the succulent hamburger; there is death in the metallic glitter of the ornaments, in the stitches of high fashion, in the products of distant plantations; there is death in the Third World, in the flow of low-priced commodities from poor to rich; there is death in the debt-bondage of the poorest countries. If we fail to feel the connections between ourselves and those far from us in place, is this not because we have equally failed to make those connections with another set of victims, increasingly far from us now in time?

5

Throughout the 1960s and 1970s, we were compelled to learn the limitations of personal liberation.

We would not want to underestimate the energies and hopes, the radical impulses of the 1960s. These, after all, gave rise to most of the significant political movements of the 1970s and beyond. What was flawed was the faith – and what an echo of the faith of those who set in motion the reforms of 1945! – that such projects and endeavours could re-shape the structures of capitalist society without themselves being radically deformed, diverted or disfigured in the process. Although we didn't actually make the connections at the time, there was an uneasy sense that the experience of gay liberation was replicating a parallel and far longer history of the Labour Movement, from its moment of greatest and most hopeful potency in 1945, through the long, slow subsequent dissolution in the decades that followed. The emancipatory project of the gay movement was familiar: an oppressed people were demanding their right to be seen and heard as full citizens, and not considered as deviants, just as the working class had demanded to be regarded as more than hands, as more than the sum of the produce of their labour. There was a conviction that long-suppressed energies would be resistless: if only we could free ourselves, then anything was possible. All human relationships would benefit from the openness and the diversity and the courage of our own example. We felt ourselves to be the standard-bearers of a new form of humanity, as well as the living pledge that our society was becoming more human. Such a role was not new to us: had we not been living pledges of something or other all our lives? This was the most exciting promise of all: not only had our previously most shaming characteristic become the focus of proud assertiveness, but we were actually now able to give our full being to the struggle. No longer merely the objects of the Labour Party's solicitude as oppressed workers, nor even of our parents' hopes as their aspiring children, we had gone beyond our emblematic function. After years of hiding behind other people's causes, of fuelling their struggles with our suppressed energies, we were now a cause ourselves, protagonists in a project which, we hoped, would send out powerful pulsations that would leave no one untouched. We had glimpsed once more the old socialist dream: that political struggle and personal transformation are part of one and the same process.

The utopian element of gay liberation came from its belief that the whole world could be changed, if only people would trust their own instincts above the proprieties of social convention. We declared that monogamous relationships were an unnecessary contsraint on the multitude of possibilities for 'relating' which every individual contained, if only he or she dared to be open to them. 'Coming out' became the central drama of personal liberation. Indeed, it expressed itself as both a political declaration and a kind of religious testimony. Our clarion call was to release the most beleaguered gays from their isolation in pit village and suburban avenue alike – even as the socialist gospel, if only proclaimed with no uncertain sound, would unfailingly rouse up the whole of the working class.

Later, we gathered with our friends, and resolved that we would return home that very weekend to our parents, and have it out with them. We would come out at home, and then report back to each other. How we exulted in the stories we had to tell afterwards! Responses had been many and varied. 'Do you think you should go and see the doctor?' or 'Get out that bloody door and never come back'; 'Does that mean you'll never give me grandchildren?'; 'Now tell me something I don't know'; 'Well it doesn't make any difference to me or your Dad, only don't go and tell Uncle Joe, he hates all that sort of thing.' Or perhaps they merely said 'Fancy that', or 'Do you want another cup of tea?' or just changed the subject. Some asked, puzzled, 'But what can two men *do* together?' Others reassured us 'Never mind, you'll get over it.' Whatever they said, it neither wounded nor dismayed. We had turned our back on our past, and the fellowship of the new life had begun.

This first revolutionary enthusiasm was not long sustained. The jealousies, rivalries, exclusivities and insecurities which were to have been abolished by the transforming power of our companionship, reappeared in the changed landscape of a swiftly generated commercial gay scene, even as the scourges that Labour had once declared extinct at its moment of coming together – poverty, unemployment, insecurity and violence – made their reappearance within the very transformations that Labour had wrought.

The failures of gay liberation were experienced as personal hurt and disappointment. That such a variety of sexual relationships was possible turned out to be not so much a celebration of the richness and depths of gay sexuality, but a direct analogue with a world in which freedom of choice meant increasingly the arbitrary selection of interchangeable products. Throwaway relationships were the counterpart of the throwaway articles on sale everywhere. Individuals were always at pains to distance themselves from the way in which others used the gay clubs and pubs (disdaining them as 'meat-markets' or 'one-night-stand pick-up joints'), even though everybody was at one time or another to be seen there. Gays quickly become a primary consumer group, whose tastes and habits prefigured those of the wider society, but in ways that gay libereration had not anticipated. These reflected nothing more than changes in capitalist patterns of consumption, which were far from any imagined alternative.

The failure of the public, political project was, of course, also lived out at the level of the individual. We turned increasingly to the consolations of money and what it could make available, rather than to the hopeful yet nebulous abstractions of solidarity, liberation and communality. It was difficult not to feel a sense of growing lassitude in the repetitiveness of encounters that didn't go anywhere, the predictability of one-night-stands, the hours of boredom both before and after any meeting with strangers, the exchange of phone numbers that would never be dialled, the small talk about birth signs, astrology, and the half-hearted inquiries about where people came from or what they did for a living. When the promised excitement of liberation failed to appear, the manufactured distractions and consolations of the disco beat and the flashing lights didn't at first appear to be such paltry substitutes. It took a while for the significance of what was happening to sink in.

Although the struggle for liberation may be a long and difficult one, there is never any doubt as to what one is seeking liberation *from*. What is sometimes less clear is what we are being liberated *into*. We were surprised to discover that the 'liberated state' required elaborate and sometimes costly compensations. Compensations for what? Compensations perhaps for the way in which the liberatory impulse is stifled and deformed as it seeks self-expression in capitalist society: for capitalist versions of emancipation leave us still fettered to its own limiting possibilities.

Such compensations come to take on their own solidity, filling the void formerly occupied by other, less material hopes. They become ritualized, they give a structure to life, they impose their own rhythms: on Friday night you go to the pub, Saturday night you pick up somebody; if he's all right, you spend Sunday with him, otherwise you say goodbye after breakfast, and spend the day ploughing through the Sunday papers, or if you have the energy, phone up friends to see if they want to see a film or go out for a drink. If you've been stood up, or if you are feeling down, you salve your injured pride by buying some new clothes, by changing your hairstyle, repackaging yourself for a more successful re-entry into the market-place. The expenditures involved came to be surrogates for less easily purchased desires, longings, or even needs. This is not to say that more enduring relationships and friendships didn't evolve out of these chance encounters, but this was only if they were sustained by energies and values other than those of the commercial culture in which they first developed. If we often felt driven by a relentless compulsion, this was perhaps because we sought to find in what was shifting and impermanent, something stable, authentic and secure; and in surrendering ourselves to these processes, we had to renounce any hope that what we were doing, and the ways in which we were doing it, represented anything that ran counter to the wider culture. Indeed, in many ways it was a microcosm of what was happening throughout society. The gay world was not, we discovered, a place apart: it was dependent upon the only world there is.

The vaunted tolerance of the 1960s and 1970s had much to do with the fact that the vast majority of people were busy with their own preoccupations, interests or obsessions. These all turned out to be versions, appropriate to their inclinations, of what was called consumer choice, but which were also, as it happened, capital's necessities. This is not to say that genuine communities of interest did not grow up, whether based on a shared sexuality, or a passion for Country and Western music, or darts, or gardening, or religious belief, or shared ethnicity, or even a common affliction – deafness or cystic fibrosis – in which people found both meaning and belonging. But such communities evolved in the absence of any wider sense of social purpose or significance. Public discourse was at this time full of talk about 'community' – community participation, community care, the gay community, community schools, community action, the ethnic community – the rhetoric, as so often, partly compensatory, for such things are rarely invoked with such passionate insistence unless they are either absent or decaying. Gay people became, at best, just another pressure group, another minority interest; and at worst, an object of that easy indifference extended to people who collected train numbers, or who dressed up in period costume to relive episodes of English history, or to any other adult indulgence in passions commonly held to be juvenile.

If the gay world became less and less satisfying, it became clear that we did not possess the resources to create another one. As time went by, the search for new stimuli, for new experiences, became translated into a quest for escape – for more exotic holidays, perhaps – leafing through gay guides which told you what the penalties were if you got caught in Jakarta, and what the age of consent was, and where the cruising grounds were on the parks and beaches of major world cities. And then, those of us who had vowed that we would never own more than we could carry in a rucksack, suddenly discovered that we had a wardrobe full of clothes, and an interior increasingly baroque, or more and more cluttered with labour-saving devices, *objets d'art*, and the detritus of arbitrary impulse purchases over the years. This material clutter is weighed down with something even heavier than its own bulky being: it has to bear a ponderous charge of symbolism, standing in for satisfactions, hopes, yearnings and needs which do not belong there. There is nothing unique about this surrogacy, for the urgent human requirements which it displaces have been exiled from their proper position in our culture; with the result that they prowl hungrily around and between the unyielding materialities which constitute our world, looking for a way in – very much as gay people sometimes wander through darkened public spaces, looking for eternal relationships with strangers.

The gay experience, far from being a frivolous and subsidiary part of our lives, has in fact been the locus of our most profound political education. It has instructed us in the most stark and painful way imaginable in the nature of capitalist society in this, its most advanced mutation. That is to say, we have been shown its power to strip away all traditional cultural and social characteristics, so that we stand exposed, with the most irreducible of our human attributes laid bare. We are defined as gay or straight, male or female, young or old, black or white; culturally bereft, raw and unprotected, deeply wounded and infinitely vulnerable. We are then confronted, if we are to survive, with the absolute necessity of buying back, redeeming through money, that which is, ought to be, ours by right, by virtue of our humanity. In other words, that which other societies – those allegedly more primitive – have given to their peoples, and which sustains both them and the society through practice and tradition and custom, has been ripped from us, in order that we might become more profitable in the world, through the exploitation of our most urgent and existential needs. Where a better society might mitigate, disperse or assuage some of the ache of our vulnerable sexuality, by cushioning it with ritual and custom, we are left nursing it as if it were a wound which is never allowed for one moment to heal, any more than others can soothe the inescapable division represented by their blackness or whiteness or maleness or femaleness or youth or age in cultural practices which take the burden from individuals, and celebrate the human sameness in which people recognize a shared predicament.

The capacity of the capitalist project to find ever-new sources of plunder is insufficiently recognized, even by some of its most implacable critics. It becomes clear that when the expropriated substance can be bought back only through money, that money has taken on a role both more profound and more sinister than that of being a mere medium of exchange. This is how money is, literally, transfigured into our life-blood, and becomes the object of such total veneration. When we realize that the further developments of late twentieth-century capitalism involve, not merely the reduction of the worker to the detail labourer (a hand), but also the reduction of all human being to a single characteristic, it should be apparent that socialists have too easily conceded the progressive nature of capitalist development. For it is one thing to release the forces sleeping in the lap of social labour, but it is quite another to imagine that the pillaging of the planet on one hand, and the gutting of the individual human being on the other – no matter what 'wealth' emerges from these rapacious processes – could ever form the basis for any humane socialist alternative.

It might be thought that our far from sentimental education had adequately prepared us for the strange forms of further education that the 1980s were going to impart. We underestimated the resourcefulness and the pedagogic capacity of the present dispensation. As the Chartists had once warned, 'a new schoolmaster is abroad in the land'. It was left for the 1980s to make clear that a group of people encouraged to identify themselves as a lucrative and distinctive market, later became vulnerable to identification by others as both a polluting and a threatening minority.

6

Whereas in the 1960s we had learned that capitalism was a benign system, under which all manner of emancipations were possible, we have been under instruction in the 1980s to realize the provisional and partial nature of our earlier forms of knowledge. Having been enticed into public acknowledgement, indeed celebration, of our previously hidden sexuality, we now discovered ourselves to be, in the words of a Christian Chief Constable, 'swilling around in a cess-pool of our own making'. From being the harbingers of transformation, we were trapped into being prototypes of those unencumbered and mobile social groups with high disposable income. Subsequently we have become the secret infectors of society, pollutants, recruiters of the young and vulnerable into an unspeakable sectarian persuasion; worse, bearers of the plague.

It was only one among many inconsistencies of the government to promote its anti-AIDS campaigns with an appeal to the people not to die of ignorance, when ignorance is one of the few commodities still in abundant manufacture in post-industrial Britian. Not the least of these engines propagating incoherence is the *Sun* newspaper, one of the most uncritical supporters of the Conservative administration. For on the very day that the crusade against AIDS was launched, the *Sun* carried the following 'news' item: 'Grim-faced ministers emerged from a Cabinet meeting, fearful that the killer plague AIDS will spark violence on the streets of Britain. The prospect of bloodshed as terrified citizens make "reprisal" attacks on homosexuals and drug addicts is now seen as a real threat. Some gays are expected to retaliate by spreading the virus to the rest of the community through "revenge sex" with bisexuals.'

Just what his Gothic scenario is calculated to contribute to the fight against AIDS is not immediately clear. Not only does the spread of superstition make it more likely that the victims of AIDS will be driven to more frantic efforts at concealment, but such 'reporting' also resuscitates antique scares associated with 'smearers', those who were believed to be deliberately infecting the population in outbreaks of plague during the Middle Ages. (Indeed, the *Sun* becomes more and more medieval each day in style as well as content. Many of its headlines sound like a parody of medieval poetry, with their rhymes and alliterations: Princess

Pushy – haughty and naughty, Naughty Night Nurse Sold Sex, Jobs Joy for Maggie, Moors Murderer Myra Must Rot, etc.)

This might at first seem an incomprehensible exercise; but it is of a piece with the purposes over a long period of much of the popular press and the so-called entertainment industries, who have set themselves up as purveyors of fantasy and horror to the people; a role perhaps more readily accepted in the vacuum created by all the ruined workplaces and the decayed and broken communities. What might once have been benignly regarded as competition in the search for sensation in order to sell newspapers is long past. It is becoming clear that the extremes of shame and degradation to which human beings are daily shown to be ready to sink, the parade of cruelties that they will commit against each other, can no longer be contained in the realm of fantasy, but strain to reinsert themselves into a social reality from which, it might have been thought, they were securely and irrevocably separated.

What we are living through is a sustained attempt to resurrect 'the mob'. The newspapers and the junk videos portray people, in the language of the *Sun*, as dirty rats and filthy swine, as animals and beasts. A vast human bestiary has been reinvented which systematically represents people as corrupt, treacherous and venal; in contrast to whom, in this simple Manichean world, the good is represented by money.

An admiring submission to the price of everything is the only morality known to the *Sun*: the sums commanded by pop stars, the cost of the mansion in Malibu, the details of the extravagant life-style of celebrities, the amount paid for the transfer of a football idol, the quantity of money earned by Bruce Springsteen in the fortnight after his new album appeared – these compel the closest thing to reverence.

The mere selling of newspapers topples over into the creation of an ideological construct, the lineaments – and the antecedents –

of which become clearer day by day. An earlier, more modest designation of people as junkies and vandals and alkies and thugs now looks relatively harmless set beside the beasts and fiends and monsters, the creatures of pure evil who inhibit the second half of the 1980s. The saga of our social life in this version is one of chaos and humiliation, of brutalization and breakdown, where you can't trust anyone further than you can see them, where everybody is out for the same thing – the sacred trinity of money, sex and fun – of which there is never quite enough to go round. In this pursuit, everything falls apart – families, relationships, friendship, trust. The only repository of faith in this bleak land-scape is hard cash.

In the same week as this particular AIDS scare, it was also reported that crime figures had reached record levels. The law and order rhetoric of eight years of Conservative rule has failed, and it is time for a further ideological turn of the screw. Considering that the economy, as they never tire of telling us, is performing better than ever before, it can only be that we are being prepared for more lurid diversions for when we shall have fallen from this privileged state. We are living in a time of confusion, of strange portents and signs; only just short of the night of the demon, when witches and devils and dragons stalk the land. At the next stage, surely the deliverer will come, St George, the bringer of order and the restorer of things. We await a millenarian deliverance.

When it is finally revealed what the 1980s have done to Britain, when not only manufacturing industry, but the benefits of oil can be seen to have deserted us, then the real asperities will start. Cuts in welfare will make even the present unhappy time look like an age of the most tender compassion. The lowering of living standards will affect not just the poor and the unemployed, but a majority of the people. Then will be the danger of the man on the white horse, the crusaders, the merchants of deliverance with their racism, homophobia and intolerance of dissent. We can already see quite clearly one outline of a possible future; and it will not come from the Left.

Just as Camus's plague bacillus lay dormant in drawers and chests and papers, waiting for the moment when it would send forth its rats to die in the unsuspecting city, so the forces for which that plague was a metaphor are stirring once more, ready to work their transformation in a Britain which is increasingly unrecognizable as the familiar and loved home-place, but looks more and more like the future site of the Second Coming of those brutalities which we went to war to defeat less than half a century ago.

7

At the deepest level, it is difficult not to feel that our lives are being used as object-lessons in a new morality play which employs the ambiguous consequences of those partial liberatory achievements of the 1960s as justification for the violent closing down and fettering that is the purpose of the 1980s, with its reimposition of old disciplines, coercions and taboos.

Indeed, the last years of the 1980s starkly illuminate the true nature of the emancipations of the 1960s that remained clouded at the time. The violence which this age has inflicted upon the sensibility formed in the 1960s has released in us – as in many others – powerful emotions which are not easily contained. To explore these inner conflicts is, at this moment, no act of personal indulgence, but a prerequisite for any serious engagement with the changed world in which we live. It is in the most personal that we shall perhaps find the most shared and common basis for a coherent response to the barbarities of which we are witnesses and victims.

How shall we best describe such painful feelings, if not by naming them?

Surprise

We feel abused and exploited by a system which gave us to believe that through us, it would itself be humanized. We were given to understand that the values which we had drawn from our own background could modify previous social cruelties, become a living part of the social organism, so that people would never again have to suffer as those we loved had suffered. We thought the world was capable of a transformation which would make central what had been at the heart of our own homes and neighbour-hoods. A profound conciliation was possible, in which the rich and powerful would acknowledge their error, would admit the delu-sive folly of their worship of money above humanity. Those who had been set over us would undergo a change of heart, and would recognize that the values they had despised and rejected as impracticable could become the informing spirit of a recon-structed social order. Our own progress in the world was evidence of this change of heart; we were the precursors of a new humanity. Our faith in this pioneering enterprise gave us the energy that we took into work with 'those less fortunate than ourselves', those in need, those temporarily (it seemed) excluded from the advantages of which we had become such conspicuous beneficiaries. Through teaching we were giving others a helping hand, in the desirable process of reproducing ourselves and the values vested in us. In social work, we were engaging upon a mission of rescue of those of our own people stranded – through no fault of their own – among the slums and poverty that still awaited abolition. In spite of our enthusiasm, we were prepared to concede that Rome had not been built in a day.

The 1980s have demonstrated how fond our hopes were. A fusion of sorts has indeed taken place between the values of the old society and the dreams we carried with us; but it has been the values of the old society that have won out. Instead of being able to gain the world for the people, it is the world that has retaken the people. When our contribution – which we can now see was to conceal the nature of the transformation that was occurring – had fulfilled its purpose, we could be spewed out, our mission of camouflage and dissimulation complete. Far from being the pathfinders of the way of liberation for the people, we have marched into a blind alley, indeed into a trap. Instead of open country, there are brick walls, and the forces of law and order are drawn up before them with truncheons raised. As we look back for support to those we hadn't doubted were following us from the underworld, we find that they have vanished, and we are left on our own to explain our trespass in this unauthorized place. Our excuses sound lame: we were misinformed, we listened to too many tall stories, we thought we had an appointment, there has been a terrible misunderstanding. All we can now ask is to be allowed to go home quietly, even though we are unsure of the way back.

Helplessness
But what can you do about it? – This question confronts the unchangeability of the way things are. It capitulates without struggle to the barbarity of the present. The paradox, of course, is that we are not alone in our helplessness; and yet that sense of aloneness is the cause of our helplessness. For so many people are expressing the same thing. It is a negative solidarity, a shared denial of the collective. In our isolation we are all the same. Up and down the country the same responses are heard, whatever evil confronts us. What can you do about it? If people are forced to seek a living rummaging through mounds of rubbish, if children are walking the streets of the cities for the purposes of prostitution, if people are frightened to give up their jobs in sweat-shops redolent of Victorian England, if parts of London at night have the aspect of a vast funeral, with hundreds of people sleeping in rows of cardboard coffins, few people will be found ready to declare

that these things are evidence of a good or just society. Rather they say 'It's not right', 'It's shameful', 'It's disgusting', 'It never ought to happen', 'Such things are a blight on civilized society', 'It's unbelievable', 'I never thought I'd live to see the day', 'It makes you wonder what this country's coming to.'

But these conversations always end with a question that has become a kind of universal last word on everything – *But what can you do about it?* This is perhaps the most widely heard interrogative of despair in Britain today.

There is, of course, a further answer to what has come to look like a merely rhetorical question. That answer also takes the form of yet another question. If there is nothing to be done about all these oppressions and afflictions, then what of the vaunted freedoms that are supposed to distinguish us from less favoured regimes and forms of government? The helplessness and impotence in the face of insupportable wrongs and inadmissible evils come from fear and unwillingness to frame that further question. Indeed, even to broach such an inquiry is to lay bare the depth and extent of our unfreedoms, the degree to which we are in thrall to the system which lives through us, and in which we live. Helplessness, for all its discomforts, has become familiar. *But what can you do about it?* has the ring of a conclusive finality that places such issues beyond the scope and ability of mere human beings. It is a response which is both infantile (we can never hope to understand) and mature (we recognize the limits of human ability to alter the way of the world). It offers us the consolation of becoming as little children, combined with the recognition of one's modest place in the order of things. This, of course, is the stuff of religion. The principal consolations of this religion have, however, the unique advantage of being almost wholly material. This is a religion nourished by no uncertain manna. If current political debate seems so vacuous, this is because it must evade the centrality of this universal impotence, which has conferred so many fragile and threatened benefits upon those who know, and do not know, what needs to be done.

Redundancy

We did not doubt that we had a significant purpose in furthering the radical social reconstruction that appeared to be taking place. And indeed, our function was crucial, although not quite in the way we imagined. We were not the ambassadors from a richer way of life but, rather, minor functionaries whose duties lay in providing a decent façade behind which the serious business of restructuring could proceed, unhindered and unobserved. Whatever our professed concern for people and their needs, our all-too-public tenderness failed to touch in any way the impersonal calculations of those whose concern remained wholly with ever new sources of profit. Our sincerity was their display. It was merely another form of the cultural window-dressing at which they have shown themselves so adept. We were human lay-figures set in stylized gestures of compassion, exalted sales personnel who were scarcely aware of what they were selling. A modelling career, that coveted ambition of so many working-class adolescents, was ours without our ever being aware of it. Though career is perhaps too strong a term; it was essentially a temporary appointment, lasting no longer than the period of transition from a traditional capitalism, naked, to one that was clothed, and in the latest fashion at that. At the end of this season, we were to be unceremoniously dismissed, given our cards, sent down the road.

Redundancy has been the misfortune, not only of those unhappy workers told on the Friday evening that the factory where they had worked for twenty years would cease operations forthwith. With them, we share the consequences and the anguish, the resentment and pain of their equally brusque ejection from the productive process. 'We thought it would be there for ever', they said, as they contemplated the mangled and twisted metal of their ruined work-place. How similar are our own feelings, as we contemplate the wreckage and the disfigurement of the apparatus of caring to which we have also given the best years of our lives. What exciting new job opportunities beckon to them, as they pound the bleak streets of the council estates, during the long days they have to ruminate upon the unappealable lessons of the market-place? And what openings for us, how shall we price ourselves back into profitable employment in a market where skills in mitigating the workings of that inhuman machinery are no longer required, or, as the current desultory attempts at euphemism describe it, 'can no longer be afforded'? How many of those excluded from work have, in despair, taken to spending half the day in bed and the other half watching endless serials on afternoon TV? And how many of us have switched off from politics, opted out, settled for the comforting tedium of private life? Like the handloom weavers, the wheelwrights and the boiler-makers, we have seen ourselves bypassed by that onward march of progress which turns out, as ever, to be nothing more than the mechanisms of profit, which grind to dust human beings and their skills with the indifference of those agencies which can command as many hands or brains or other parts of the human anatomy as they may require for their business.

Exile

Britain has traditionally been famed for its hospitality to political refugees from less favoured lands. As the twentieth century has advanced, this generosity has diminished, perhaps in anticipation of a time when the country would have exiles enough of its own. That moment has now come. In Britain, exile doesn't mean Gorki or Patagonia, but for all that, what we are experiencing is a form of internal exile. The long descent inwards, the retreat from public life, the withdrawal from any social hope have come about because we feel that we are inhabiting a foreign country. We have travelled nowhere, yet our position resembles that of those who have travelled vast distances. In the 1950s and 1960s large numbers of black people, also servants of an expanding economy, looked to see the life-chances of their children extend in ways their own servitude had denied them. Those former migrants of hope now find themselves hostages in a hostile land, where their presence is regarded as an embarrassment and an obscure reproach to the greedy workings of an economy which sucked them in and then expelled them with such violence, leaving their children even more dispossessed than they were. Theirs is a crueller exile, from which there is no going back, and yet so little going forward either. We can feel our kinship with them as never before in a land that has been rendered alien, not by their presence and their pain, but by the workings of those same iron laws that have used us all up and then discarded us, leaving us to take responsibility for the consequences of its global operations and the people it destroys. It leaves us all perpetual strangers, pierced by longings for a home that does not exist, a journey which can never be undertaken, a belonging that has been irreparably broken.

Disappointment

We imagined that we were partly instrumental in bringing about a society which we might have had faith in, could have felt glad to give ourselves to. It wouldn't have mattered how limited our functions were, if we had not felt that our energies were being confiscated or ripped off for other purposes. Working in adult education, in social work, in schools, in public administration, ought to have yielded rewards other than the wage packet, whether those rewards belonged to us or to our pupils or clients. The haloing of these undertakings led us to believe that they would enhance the lives of those they touched, that they would offer something beyond the improvement of their market position.

For us as teachers there were, of course, consolations beyond the salary cheque, but not in the form we had hoped and expected. Those consolations were of raised status and the deference of those we served as role-models. And yet, we could not help perpetuating the same myths by which we had been deluded. We had thought that there existed a being called the 'educated person', one whose inner life was enriched and who, in consequence, spread a pool of enlightenment and civility in the circles among which she or he lived and worked. There had been less evolved examples of this in our childhood – the trade union official, or political party member, or local preacher, who had both by example and instruction been a powerful force within the community. In other words, education bore a potential transforming power (still sometimes deferred to in professional clichés about releasing the potential of every human being) which was spiritual in nature, a form of grace, a promise of transcendence. Why these qualities are no longer sought in that particular realm is clear: they have deserted it for more suitable contemporary dwelling-places. For what education once gestured towards, money now promises to deliver. Is it any wonder that teachers, like preachers, and other servants of the life of the spirit, tend to feel baffled, cheated and disappointed?

If there were non-material rewards to be had from these ministrations, our experience was that they resided in the admiration of the young, in the regard and emulation of the untutored. On the first morning of the term there was still an eagerness and excitement which, we always knew, were doomed to change into something else before many years had passed. We were tormented and incapacitated by the knowledge (which had nothing to do with learning) that what we had to pass on could not transform their lives in the ways that they might have hoped, any more than that knowledge had enabled us to make the whole-hearted contribution which we had wanted to make to the emancipation of our own people. Thus the compensations of the teacher's life took on a primordial importance. The only true moment of elation in the staff-room occurred towards the end of July, as people prepared to depart for ever more exotic destinations, and a visit to Greece became a substitute for that life of the mind which was never realized at school. Our failings and disappointments could be read in a magisterial disdain for the pupils, the 'no-hopers', on whose reports were scribbled 'could do better', 'must try harder'; the suppressed message being that no matter how much better they did, or how much harder they tried, the best they could ever hope to achieve was the ambiguous and deceitful status that we had attained.

How we longed to pass on something of real value, other than the dictated notes on the six causes of the French revolution, or the tragic flaw in Hamlet's character. What on earth might that have been? It might have meant transmitting an understanding of the terms of human existence, and an insight into the diverse shapes into which it is moulded by different societies in the world. We would have liked to share with our pupils the inescapability of suffering and laughter, of fear, desire, mortality and joy, and to have shown how these human experiences are handled in other cultures, as well as in our own. Such a venture would, of course, have required forms of wisdom that have been suppressed, and which have been reordered to appear only fitfully as commodities purveyed by counsellors, experts and agony aunts.

Such specialization is, of course, all part of an extreme and minute subdivision of labour, a labour of the intellect which has become as discrete and unintelligible as the meaninglessly repeated tasks of the detail labourer in the early industrial period. At no point in the process does the work have to make sense. The role of the teacher has been fragmented and dispersed into multiple employments, leaving teachers as mere supply-systems of a glut of information which will ensure a continuing bemusement of its recipients, and their separation from any understanding of how it is all connected. To speak of a wholehearted commitment, indeed to speak of a whole any-thing in such a profession, let alone in the society of which it is such a characteristic expression, would be very difficult.

If we have been disappointed by a more diminished function than that which we had anticipated in this sometime noble enterprise, our disappointments are compounded by the lack of any significant resistance to what has become the promotion of universal incoherence rather than enlightenment. In the 1980s teachers feel themselves impoverished, their status undermin-ed, their expectations cheated. If this expresses itself in pay disputes, strikes and militancy, it is because their position as subordinate functionaries has been made amply clear to them; and as for any other such workers, money is the only means of making up for the absence of deeper satisfactions. This is why, when their opponents accuse them of abandoning high princi-ples, of betraying their calling, of departing from standards of professional conduct, they remain unmoved. For they sense that it is not *they* who have betrayed the children, it is not *they* who have set down the terms on which the society sees fit to conduct its business. On the contrary, those who are most noisy about the lowering of standards, about the lack of discipline, about teachers failing their students, are the very same people who have preached the necessity of our fullest subservience to the ethics of the market-place. Those who attack the teachers most vigorously for their shortcomings and lack of professional commitment are the very same who preside over a system which makes money and profit the ultimate arbiters of morality. No wonder they seek alibis for the painful human con-sequences of their own blind faith. No wonder they seek scapegoats on whom they can heap the blame that is properly theirs. What greater disappointment could there be than being compelled to witness each day the damage done by these developments?

If there is such faint resistance, this is because the teachers, like so many other workers, have been caught up in economic and social structures which they fear to challenge, because any such challenge might result in the loss and withdrawal of the benefits which the system so palpably makes available. It is such benefits which make our own lives appear so much richer than the lives both of previous generations, and of people in other societies, but which can be sustained only by *unknowing*. Those who have claimed that their task is to defend the best interests of the people – the Labour Movement – have also fallen conspicuously silent on these contradictions. Is it because they long ago decided that a direct challenge to these compromises and collusions might lay bare the deeper corruption at the core of the system which their reforms have served so long to conceal? There is nothing special about *our* disappointment: it goes wide and deep, and it may well be that others are expressing the same disappointment when they declare their disaffection from politics, and their belief that there is nothing to choose between any of the political parties. What people are saying is that they feel powerless to exert any influence over the shape or the direction of the democracy which is supposed to serve them.

Dividedness

In spite of an inability to commit ourselves to present forms of social progress, there is still a yearning to belong, to be part of some group which is involved in something indisputably good. Although this society in many aspects may be cruel and ugly, there is no other at hand. We are like Wordsworth's protagonists in convulsive changes in eighteenth-century France, who

> Were called upon to exercise their skill,
> Not in Utopia, subterraneous Fields,
> Or some secreted island, Heaven knows where,
> But in the very world which is the world
> Of all of us, the place in which, in the end,
> We find our happiness, or not at all,

The Prelude, Book 10, 723–8

The retreat into private life is always tempting. Indeed, in the last few years, the private life has been presented to us all as the way of salvation. Mrs Thatcher has even gone as far as to say (in October 1987) that there is no such thing as society, there are merely individuals and their families. But this is never enough. More, the flight into private life only exacerbates the evil you are fleeing, not least because our private lives are themselves the site of some of the fiercest contradictions of society. As we flee to the sanctuary of individual solutions, we find this refuge already invaded by tensions and conflicts which can find resolution and meaning only through participation in a shared project. Meaning and mutuality go together; they are not a choice. If they seem to have become so, this is a measure of the disorder in society which reproduces in us its own contradictions. There are, of course, those who, on the other hand, seek to find in the public sphere, or in Utopian politics, or in the religious life, a ready solution for personal pain. This is a project as vain as that dictated by the existing culture, which forces us through the thwarting of every variation of public hope, until we are prepared to accept that the only satisfactions available to us are to be sought in the private sphere.

This feeling of dividedness is perhaps most clearly focused by the idea of *home*, and where home is. For people without children, this is more clearly poignant than for those who have recreated a family structure of their own. For us, the question is why are we in London and not in Blackburn and Northampton? Why do we still, even in our forties, talk about 'going home'? As parents become older and more frail, the reasons for not being with them have to be more compelling; and yet, unencumbered by family obligations (which of course, can serve both as a real reason, as well as an excuse, for absences and neglects), what binding ties can we point to to explain the absences that are always just a little too long, the visits that are always just a little too short? 'You have your own life to lead', they say, with a generosity based, perhaps, upon the fear that a straight demand might meet with a less straight, but equally clear, refusal. And what of this life of ours to which they defer? What is the nature of the relief we feel on leaving the home town? 'You can't come here to look after us', they say, not formulating the real question, which is, how it is that all our lives have been constructed in such a way that to do just that is inconceivable, even though it is obvious that to be looked after is their greatest need? The most acceptable reason for our prolonged absence is economic. Work. This calls upon deep and older traditions: the necessity of going out early in the morning, the workman's ticket and the tramping boots; although many years ago they used to say 'Why don't you get yourself a real job?' or 'You don't know the meaning of work' or 'You've never done a proper day's work in your life.' The changed response to the nature and significance of our labour is a measure of the role it now has to play in legitimizing our staying away.

And yet, being absent is painful in a different way from being there. For one thing, the caring services, in which we had placed so much faith, are not adequate; nor, perhaps could they ever be. (Those who say that if only the welfare state were sufficiently funded we would have the good society, are wrong: it would still not be the good society, although it would be a better one.) Our families have been doubly bereft in their lifetime. They have lost not only the extended network of kin, but even the more threadbare comforts of the nuclear family as well. When they complain that no one ever comes across the threshold, what they are really saying is that there are no longer enough people surrounding them to sustain a human life. For they, as we, are pioneers in advanced forms of individualism: the furthest extension of which may be a society in which nobody can bear to live with anyone else. Already one-quarter of the households in Britain consist of only one person. (This may be tough on the people, but what a bonanza for those who deal in personal services as commodities.) To know that they have been at the forefront of these developments affords scant consolation to those who still carry memories of high days and holidays when the parlour was so full that they had to borrow chairs from next door so that everybody could sit down to tea together.

For us, London was always a place of escape; escape, apparently, from the necessity of following the family into the staple industries of our towns (textiles and leather); although such necessity had already been removed by changes in the employment structure of those industries (which required far less labour than ever before), as well as by the actions of our parents who, perhaps sensing these changes, vowed that their sons would never go into the mill or factory. Our own sense of these economic mutations expressed itself in the urgent desire to flee the niggling and relentless probing of kin into what we were coming to regard as our private lives. They thought they were entitled to say 'When are you going to find a nice girl and settle down?' 'When are you going to start a family of your own?' We thought this was an unwarrantable intrusion into those less acceptable relationships we hoped to discover in due course, although we were not sure how this was to happen.

Life at home was claustrophobic, trivial, predictable. We knew that we didn't have to accept their version of life. Their wisdom appeared antique, their knowledge redundant, their experience irrelevant. There was an overwhelming relief in not having to answer to anyone, in the haven of public indifference to whatever you did in London. This seemed a more than adequate reward for making the effort to leave home. It even felt like an act of courage, the next step in making a life of our own. Our escape was attended by the excitement of all the people we would meet, of the kind of relationships that defied the narrow classifications of our provincial town, relationships which we had read about in novels – not all of them 'set texts'. Perhaps we would even be taken up by glamorous people who would recognize our talent, our sensitivity, our superior understanding of the world, people whom we would entertain and amaze with our revelations of a Northern life which, at that time, appeared to be enjoying a brief vogue.

This desire for personal growth and development was necessary and positive. It doesn't have to be a doomed enterprise, although now we can see that within the possibilities made available to us, this could never have been satisfactorily accomplished. It is always necessary to leave home in order to grow up; but when the home of origin and the home of destination are equally inadequate, you have to ask whether the project of growing up is possible. Why is the choice between the stifling, the over-intense, the limited on the one hand, and the dispersed, the thin, the indifferent and the meaningless on the other? Both remain falsely opposed, suppressing the possibility of a true reconciliation, leaving us to oscillate between the two illusory alternatives, perpetually dissatisfied and constantly unfulfilled.

There is a further division. There are aspects of both half-worlds which we are able to use to our own personal advantage in this life (and in this life, what other kind of advantage is there to be sought?). In one place we appear, deceptively, as representatives of the real world of labour and rootedness; in the other, as emissaries of a fuller, richer life. This is all mere appearance; the truth is the reverse – the emptiness inside. As so often in advanced capitalist society, the joys and pleasures are all to be sought on the surface, while the pain and the penalties are within, concealed from view. These restless dualisms are in part imposed by the way society is fundamentally structured, and in part chosen by us as a way of dealing with the world. But what kind of choice is it to which no alternative is offered?

Loathing

Loathing maybe distinguished from hatred if hatred is directed at individuals. What we loathe is the system of values which has once more gained ascendancy during the 1980s. It long predated these years, of course, but it has perhaps never been so triumphalist as it is now. We loathe that *hatred* of the poor which forbears to express itself in such direct terms, but is rather revealed in a sensibility whose sole expression of tenderness is for the public purse, to which it feels it has contributed disproportionately. Its resentment of taxation really means 'Let the poor do as we have done, or let them perish.' We loathe the self-satisfaction of those who call themselves 'independent' when they mean rich. We loathe the intolerance which would deny existence to all those who do not make money, as they have made money, and whose sole humanitarian concession is that there may be those unable to do so by reason of visible and physical affliction, like the blind and the war-wounded. We loathe that artificial construction of a 'real world' in which they compel us all to live. We loathe the 'practical common sense' which insists that we must all live within our means, even when the survival of the system they cherish with such reverence has depended absolutely upon borrowed money, mortgaged time, deferred payment, inexhaustible credit, the per-petual postponement of the day of reckoning to the very crack of doom. Such 'common sense' is above all, deeply unkind, since it sees health and well-being as attributes of an impersonal system rather than as needs of human beings. And yet, it still feels it necesssary to cloak itself in the language of caring: Of course we

all want more hospitals and welfare, but you can't achieve these
good things until you get enough money; and you can never get
enough money if you deny the people who create wealth the
incentives to go on making enough for themselves; and they can
never have enough, because the system they serve depends upon
more and more, and upon enough remaining always insufficient.
Therefore there can never be adequate hospitals and welfare,
unless people pay for these things themselves; while the rest make
their own accommodation with sickness and death – and this will
provide a suitable spectacle of instruction to the rest. The system
seeks to render what is perfectly intelligible, if brutish, an
impenetrable phenomenon, surrounded by mysteries too profound for our comprehension; in other words, to make us accept it
as though it were our fate, even our destiny. As its workings have
become more extended and have struck deeper roots all over the
world, this process of obfuscation and sanctification becomes
easier; and this is the key to its triumph at this time. The simple
parables about savings and thrift and prudence and enterprise are
all camouflage, as greater and greater concentrations of wealth
move over the earth independently of these homely and comforting truths.

Even less pardonable is the pretence that these processes have
any reference to the country to which their representatives pro-
claim such clamorous patriotic devotion. Home is where the
money is; and money is where it can beget more of itself,
unhindered by national statutes and legislation, nesting in enterprise zones and off-shore havens, duty-free areas and trans-
national entities, parastatal corporations, movable enclaves with
no geographical existence. And the zealots who serve and protect
these nebulous migrations of money call themselves patriots! In
truth, the servitors of capital have no country – unlike working
men and women who are, alas, all too bound to theirs – but are the
international camp-followers of profit, at home everywhere and

nowhere, risking their all in the endless war against humanity for the sake of the looting and plunder to be had.

We who grew up under the impression that our country had won the war and successfully resisted foreign domination, have had to learn that such was not the case. It is not just that Britain has fallen under foreign domination – for foreigners are, after all, human beings – but has passed into the alien control of a global wealth and power to which we are all equally disposable. While we were more than grateful to relinquish the destructive burdens of empire, we did not think that thereby we had given up the right to manage the affairs of our own territory. Yet we have lived to see the transfer of production from factories in our home towns, where our parents struggled for better wages and decent conditions, to the sweatshops of Taipei and Seoul and Manila and São Paolo. And we have been told that such decisions are rational and unappealable; and even if they are not, there is nothing we can do about it. Indeed, it is suggested, our modest efforts to humanize the world of work in Britain are precisely what has caused the workplaces to desert the familiar landscapes of our sometime industrial towns and cities.

Fear

We are afraid of how far it all might go, and what they might do to us in order to compel our acquiescence. We are afraid of the thinness of the veneer of civility that overlies the barbarities that are daily taking place. We are afraid of how deeply rooted the values of the system are in the hopes and fears of the people; of how the ideology – the faith – in capitalism in its present mutation sustains and gives meaning to people's lives. To the extent to which the people have become dependent upon the satisfactions afforded by the existing economic structures, the people are our potential enemies, and can be mobilized against us, dissenters and spoilers, indeed unbelievers. As most dissenters have always claimed, we feel that we are the true bearers of an older and more authentic faith; we must, and do, expect persecution. We wonder whether this will take the form of being penalized for omitting our proper devotions; or whether it will come to being paraded before our own funeral pyre, as has happened to the adherents of older, supplanted religions; or whether irresistible pressure will be applied that will encourage us to recant, as others have done before us, when shown the instruments of persuasion.

Of course all this may be seen as apocalyptic, over the top, too extreme. The fabric of our society is more resilient than we allow for, we are told. After all, are not tolerance and decency the finest qualities of the British people? Yes; but that was before the bringers of the good news set up their pulpits in the market-place, before the time of mass conversions, the wholesale apostasies. We ought not to put too much reliance on British – or any other – decency, if it were required to stand up to the full rigour of global pressures – the falling living standards, the sudden scarcities, the withdrawal of credit, the bank failures and, most sombre of all, a future without money. Even while the economy is 'in good health', the stories filter out from the poor enclaves in the inner cities and the outer estates: the outrages against children, women, black people; the sagas of fire-bombings and revenge killings, the gang fights, the drug wars, the rape of old women, the random woundings. These give us some inkling of how it might be should the economy 'take sick'. It would not be difficult to imagine a cowed and frightend citizenry entering Tesco's under armed guard, exercising their diminished consumer freedoms in the shadow of half-empty shelves. It is not so far from the images of crowds on the streets of Third World cities with handkerchiefs over their faces as the canisters of gas explode all around them. How far is that anyway from the burning of Brixton, the occupation of Broadwater Farm, the looting of Debenhams in provincial high streets on Saturday afternoons, the football wars?

We are afraid that when the current government's policies falter, only a move to the more authoritarian Right will seem plausible. This is not based upon any pessimistic estimate of human nature, or any lack of faith in the people, but is a measure of the depth of penetration of people's sensibilities by the values of a system that cannot permit any alternative to itself, and which has successfully persuaded us that any deviation from its own necessary evolution must bring loss, chaos and violence. For we are living under a system which translates all that is into its own terms, and renders unintelligible all other languages and dialects. At all the places in the world where men and women gather hangs the sign Money Spoken Here. Anything that resists translation into this universal medium can have no voice, indeed must be silenced; and those who would continue to employ any other antique discourse must be brought by the hard way to see the benefits of a common tongue. Money has become the great leveller. Of course, there have always been those who have denounced money and its dominance in human life. We have constantly been warned against the power of money to engulf feelings and emotions; it was a temptation to be guarded against. What we now see is not human beings tempted by the love of gold, but their inability to extricate themselves from its compulsions; the lack of certainty where what may be purchased ends and what is freely given begins; indeed, whether the freely given can continue to exist at all.

We fear that in the process of future retrenchment, there will have to be human sacrifice. The names of the victims are familiar. They are always the cause of the woes visited upon the people; whether they were seen anointing the door-jambs of houses with plague, or whether they were known to cast the evil eye upon a neighbour's cows which sickened and died; or whether they drank the blood of Christian babies; or whether they cast lascivious glances upon the the unsullied women of the tribe.

Individuals have always feared that the world would be eclipsed for all time by their death; that they would one day have to look for the last time upon the sky and the familiar landscape. But the possibility that no one will ever see those things again is a new world fear – a fear not so much of accident as of willed action: for we fear that those who possess the wealth and power of the world would rather see the world destroyed than abandon one particle of their riches. People doubt that; but one must remember that the rich are those who know all about human nature, indeed are the most inflexible proponents of its selfishness, greed and venality. We must assume that they are speaking from their own experience, installed, perhaps not quite beyond hope of rescue, at the centre of their riches.

Unhappily, even if their wishes are granted, and industrial society, capitalist or socialist, goes on growing and expanding for ever, there will sooner or later be conflict over the dwindling resources which alone permit such expansionism; and that will lead to the same unhappy fate as that predicted by Marx as a result of the *internal* contradictions of the system, i.e. the ruin of the contending classes. If humanity is to survive, the rich must renounce their version of riches; it is perhaps our greatest fear that they will not do so.

Self-doubt

The possibility remains that our opponents might, after all, be right. Infinite growth and constant expansion may be the most certain guarantors of the continuation of freedom and variety in the world; such a process may be sustainable for ever. It is possible that human ingenuity will overcome resource depletion; that the poor will all benefit from a vast increase in the wealth of the rich. Perhaps the pain and the anxiety that many of us feel *are* just individual disorders after all, the results of faulty nurture or tainted blood (and who can claim to be free of either of those?). Perhaps we just didn't have the courage to compete, to take what we wanted for ourselves when the going was good, confusing cowardice with virtue. It may be that we can't accept the world as it is, or at least as they say it is. There is certainly evidence that the belief of the Left in social redemption has been naïve. It is true that wars and violence have been endemic in recorded human experience. It is true that a majority of humankind have given little thought for anything beyond the moment in which they are living; and this is as true of those on the very edge of subsistence as of those who have never had their slightest whim denied. Perhaps most people have always been afraid of change except in the most dire circumstances, prepared to put up with almost anything as long as it is familiar. Most have accepted serfdom, oppression, bonded labour, dispossession of their own land. It may be true that the vast majority is insensitive to the sufferings of others, not from ignorance, but consciously. It may be that if we look inwards with sufficient clarity, we might discern there the same characteristics of a human nature which our opponents declare universal. Aren't we also selfish, greedy and eager for gain, in whatsoever rarefied form our particular sensibilities dictate? Is not the true source of our anger the feeling that we have not inherited our place in the sun, for which we were being so elaborately prepared, it seemed, in our youth? Isn't it that we feel pushed aside, stranded, our virtues unrecognized, perishing, as the less fit deserve to? Does not our sense of being the bearers of an alternative tradition now stand revealed as a false moral superiority, a debased aristocratic disdain for the things of everyday life, a failed calling to superior avocations which none has recognized? Isn't it possible that we are the archaic monuments to a superseded and specific moment of the history of the working class, which we have foolishly mistaken for a universal human impulse towards a different kind of society, in which sharing and mutuality would be dominant? May it not be a thwarted longing to reproduce ourselves which makes us cling to an ossified set of values which partly characterized our childhood, and which we now would wish to perpetuate at the level of ideology, having been unable to do so at the level of biology – seeking to recreate ourselves through values that have passed away, rather than through our own children?

These personal feelings – contradictory, embarrassing, incomplete – are nevertheless the roots of political passions and commitments. It is the absence of the energy and complexity of such sentiments from political discourse that makes it so unsatisfactory and superficial. If it seemed to an earlier generation that the problem was no longer to understand the world but to change it, this was because the understanding appeared to be complete, the analysis carried to its furthest limits. However, when that understanding fails, changing the world becomes an even more remote possibility, almost an evasion. The task of our generation must be to recuperate and revivify an understanding that has become hardened and formulaic. It is no longer worth arguing over the meaning of words, when those words have lost the power to move, or no longer seem to do justice to the felt experience. In other words, politicians have only changed the world in various ways; the point now is to understand it afresh in the light of the changes they have wrought.

PART TWO
Faiths

8

One of the major changes in late twentieth-century capitalism has been a radical modification of the role played by religion in sustaining the social system. For the decay of more traditional forms of the spiritual life seems to have released people's energies and feelings to seek equivalent satisfactions in other areas of human activity. In our period, capitalism has found in this free-floating religiosity, which is characterized above all by desires for transcendence and communion, new marketing opportunities. If we would understand the power of contemporary capitalism, its hold on the minds of the people, we need to examine the changing relationship between capitalism and religion. That socialism, the major critique of capitalism, is also formed on a religious structure of thought, renders the task of examination more complex.

Socialists have always been concerned with analysing religion, usually for the ostensible purpose of liberating themselves and their people from its baleful and controlling power; though, paradoxically, much of socialism's persuasive force has derived from religious structures of feeling and even, at times, from religious imagery.

This ambiguity is seen nowhere more clearly than in Marx's version of socialism. Marx is scornful of religion, though he pays tribute to its centrality. Thus, for Marx, '(The) criticism of religion is the premiss of all criticism.' It is, however, important to realize that his analysis of religion is more subtle than he is normally given credit for. If, for him, religion is 'the opium of the people', it is also 'the expression of real distress and the protest against real distress'. If Marx wishes us to give up the consoling power of religion, it is not that we should be disconsolate in the world, but that we should live in a world where we do not require consolation.

Nothing more fantastic could be conceived: and this has been one of the most disabling inheritances of the Marxist patrimony. For socialism has constantly blurred the contours that separate what is socially changeable from what is existentially unalterable. It is as though the industrial smokestacks of socialist rhetoric had obscured with smoke the shining city which might have lain beyond, as surely as the lurid imagery of the city walls of jasper and gold distracted the bedazzled spirit from what might have been possible here on earth. Both religion and socialism postulate, admittedly at a time and in a place that are at variance, the existence of a terrestrial paradise. Indeed, medieval scholars debated its precise topography (was it really at the antipodes of Jerusalem?) with the same fervour and erudition that Marxist scholars have sought its locus in the hopes and endeavours of the working class.

Marx was sensible of the assuaging powers of religion, and if he rejected its offer of liberation, this was because he wished to clear the ground for a more genuine and tangible emancipation. Thus, 'criticism has plucked the imaginary flowers from the chain not so that man will wear the chain without any fantasy or consolation, but so that he will shake off the chain and cull the living flower'. This is a deeply stirring humanistic, almost mystical vision, from which nearly all forms of socialism, even those which formally repudiate Marx, gain a borrowed strength and power. It is only when socialism begins dogmatically to dispense with this visionary energy that its programme becomes lifeless and mechanistic, indeed soulless. Socialism's determined and wilful reducing to rubble of all other worlds save that to be constructed in its own secular hereafter, has banished the spirit which gave it birth.

For its part, capitalism has been guilty of no such dogmatic folly. It is true, of course, that capitalism had to undermine religion in order that it might make its own way in the world, as R. H. Tawney has shown in *Religion and the Rise of Capitalism*. Tawney describes the confusion of the practical man during the period of transition in the sixteenth-century: 'A century before, he had practised extortion and been told that it was wrong; for it was contrary to the law of God. A century later, he was to practise it and be told that it was right; for it was in accordance with the law of nature.' Tawney shows how Puritanism, by its fervid insistence on individual salvation, retreated from the medieval ideal of a society whose ordering sought to reflect the laws of God, laws which subordinated economic activities to a higher social purpose (which was nothing less than the development of the human soul). The unforeseeable consequence of this shift in religious sensibility was to expand the realm of economic preoccupations until they became, first of all autonomous ('It is the function of the church to save souls, not to meddle in politics'), and then dominant.

In our time, capitalism, having emancipated itself from the constraints of religion, has not been content to discard them once and for all; but has wondered whether such useful adornments might not be profitably refurbished for more than ceremonial use in the new world it has created. Capitalism in the past, as Marx pointed out, has not been slow to draw upon religious tradition in order to use it as a form of social control and to justify its own values and disciplines. However, it is in contemporary capitalism that a new use of religion may be seen. In the second half of the twentieth century, capitalism has ingested the feelings and forms of religion, so that these seem immanent, dwelling within the very productive power of capitalism itself. Thus capitalism comes to appear not the antagonist or mere ally, but the avatar of religion. This means that not only do its own necessities strike the people as the very grounding realities of life, as written into the structure of the cosmos, but also that grace and beatitude are only possible through its own transactions (by means of money). One crucial effect of this has been that capitalism is no longer even seen as an economic system, far less as one possible system among others, but has come to be felt as total reality. The all-pervasiveness and omnipotence of money is the triumphal mark of its universal sovereignty.

9

That money has become a universal enabling agent is not new, any more than that the worship of money has been deplored as idolatry. Jesus warned of the danger of serving money, for, he said, 'Where your treasure is, there will your heart be also.' Shakespeare wrote of gold that

> ... This yellow slave
> Will knit and break religions, bless the accursed.

Marx's comment on this is that money is both the visible deity and the universal whore. The intensification of what has been lamented as an aberration into, first of all, the norm, and then into the source of all meaning in human life is what is occurring in our age. When people say 'You can't do anything without money', they mean that the centrality and dominance of money has exhausted many non-monetary transactions in daily intercourse. The experience of contemporary life has been the passage into monetized forms of more and more areas formerly closed to them. Just as pre-cash economies in the colonial period had to be transformed into revenue-yielding raw materials and crops, so those areas of what have always been regarded as private life, the very sanctuaries of what was basically too valuable to be purchased by money, are now the object of intensive cultivation and marketing.

Old people still sometimes assert, to universal derision, that they made their own enjoyment. What they mean is that they can

recall a time when certain activities had not yet been fully exposed
to the total attention of the market-place, which was then content
to leave the people outside working hours to such trivial activities
as playing under the lamplight at hide-and-seek, or on chalked
hop-scotch signs on the pavement, skimming stones across the
water, singing rhymes, going for walks, indeed spending whole
days in the country or by the canal, fishing with a piece of wood
and a bent pin, making trolleys and flat-waggons, playing with
conkers hardened in the oven, bluebelling, mushrooming, black-
berrying; doing turns, or singing together, with nothing more than
a mouth organ, or comb and paper accompaniment. Such juvenile
occupations existed undisturbed outside the cash economy, even
within living memory. They can now be seen to have been
profitless activities in every sense. Of course, the market economy
had already created music hall and cinema, pulp fiction, mass-
circulation newspapers, and of course, the brewing industry, to
supplement and supplant these homely diversions. These have
been more efficiently exploited to become the leisure and entertainment industries of our time, none of which can be enjoyed
without the necessary expenditure. If it were merely a question of
wonderful new experiences which are rather expensive, and
therefore out of reach of the pockets of large numbers of people,
that would be sad for the unprivileged, and an inequality to be
remedied. But it means more than that. It means not only that
things which cost money are of greater worth, but that things
which do not are first of all marginalized, and then elided;
rendered ridiculous and hence seen as having no value.

This process may be seen everywhere, and nowhere more
clearly than in the answering of basic human needs, upon which a
vast, elaborate and expensive edifice has been constructed, for the
adding of value and the extracting of profit. For instance, the
preparing and cooking of food has been to a considerable degree
superseded by the selling of prepared or convenience foods. One

doesn't have to sentimentalize the importance of people who love each other eating together, with the sharing of food being symbolic of less material kinds of nourishment, to be troubled by the extent to which people are being fed by vast corporations, and can be seen eating out of red-striped cartons or Big Mac containers as they wander through the shopping centres. The increasing remoteness of the people from the source and origin of their sustenance is only a further extension of the operations of the food processing industry, which long ago separated the majority of the population from any part in the production of their own food, and consequently from any contact with growing things. The ostensible virtue of these developments is that they release people (overwhelmingly women) from drudgery and unappreciated subservience. Women have been offered thereby a form of emancipation, of which the labour market has been the beneficiary. Women escaping from the claustrophobic confinement of the home into work say 'It gives me independence', 'I feel free', 'I feel I have a contribution to make'. Such relief as they experience is certainly felt as a liberation. What it takes no account of, however, is our increased dependence upon the money they earn, which becomes essential for the buying of things such as fast foods in the place of the slower foods that were prepared at home. What were once called meals are now renamed by an eager advertizing industry 'eating episodes'.

A further effect of this has been to summon into employment a new group of people who are, for the most part, ill-paid, non-unionized, casualized, female, young and black. That the formerly unpaid labour of women should have been brought into the public sphere may be accounted an advantage. But behind them whole populations suffer unseen. For the fabrication of meat for the fast food chain not only takes over land from former subsistence farmers, but also uses animals as food-processing factories to convert cereals into meat, thus adding value to the expensive hamburgers which the rich of the world want to eat; and an army of ghosts are dispossessed in the process. In this way, the innocent birthday treat for children in the shiny hamburger parlour becomes a feast of unwitting cannibals: our own children are learning to devour the substance of the poor of the earth.

There is nothing like a lot of money to wash the brain of all memory of how to do things without money, or with less money. Indeed, money is perhaps the most effective brain-washing mechanism of all. People who, first of all, fall out of practice of doing things themselves, then forget, then no longer know how to, are singularly at the mercy of those who would not only sell back to them the forefeited expertise, but would also exploit them in countless other ways. The purchase itself replaces the knowledge of how to create what was purchased. In addition, it eliminates all knowledge of the conditions in which the bought object or service was created. It is a double unknowing. The first shedding of the burden of knowledge renders us more dependent not only upon the flow of goods, but more especially upon the flow of money that alone will gain access to them; and thus we are welded ever more deeply into the system. The second unknowing means that we must aquiesce in whatever barbarities may be necessary to keep the process unfolding. We know that we don't know; but we have to collude with that unknowing, and dismiss our own sense of powerlessness, troubling though it may be, especially in those areas of our life where we long to be able to influence what are increasingly mysterious and unbiddable circumstances. In this way, ignorance gives us a place to rest, even though the sleep may be unrefreshing and haunted by strange shadows.

For it is not only our every waking moment that is the object of intensive market cultivation. Sleep itself is not exempt from the same processes and imperatives. First of all, whole industries are dedicated to putting us to sleep, to say nothing of the waking narcosis of television and much of the entertainment industry.

Apart from the constant inventiveness of the pharamaceutical companies, there are herbal pillows and the 'natural' products of health food shops – passiflora, valerian compound, and the elixirs to send children to sleep; the music centre, the soft lighting, those beds, sprung separately, which promise that you 'can sleep together but dream alone'. Then there are the things you take to bed, the images for the nourishment and stimulus of tired fantasies. Nor is there any need to waste these hours of unconsciousness. At the same time, you can learn how to give up smoking, nail-biting or bed-wetting, or you can learn to speak a foreign language. Alternatively, you can store up your dreams to share with your therapist. The bedchamber is deeply penetrated (if that isn't too indelicate a word) by the sex industry, another unexpected development in the division of labour. The marital aids, the split-crotch panties and the kinky underwear, the sex manuals and therapists' advice, *The Joy of Sex* on the table, vibrator in the drawer, the search for new ways of turning each other on, the decor in which all this performance (and performance is crucial) must occur, have all opened up unexpectedly profitable markets. There could be no more profound a transformation from the traditional British sleeping-place, austere and functional, with its ice-flowers on the windows in the morning, its stone hot-water bottle wrapped in a towel, the slightly sweet smell of pee in the po under the bed, the moth-balls in the bedding-box and the lumpy flock mattress. These were punitive and puritanical places, where you went only at night, and only to sleep. They have been abruptly transformed into warm all-enveloping stage sets, where the most significant encounters of our private lives unfold, troubled only by the anxiety that the sex won't be good enough for us or for our partner, the ultimate orgasm never attained, as we check the number of Capital Doctor or the agony column, if it turns out to be as unsatisfying as it seems to have been lately.

The domestic interior has become an increasingly expensive

and well-equipped refuge from the world. The only irony is that the world has got there before you, and at the heart of the private is our deepest encounter with capitalist ideology. No wonder we flee to our therapists, or hasten to find an escape route from this escapism, leaving behind the wreckage of broken personal lives strewn over a wide area, disasters caused by the malfunctioning of the only components which can be admitted to be defective – the human machines.

Nowhere has the market-place been more fundamentally invasive than in the begetting of children, the very perpetuation of the species. What simpler people might have thought to be the gift of life has become, for this society, a matter of much calculation. 'We'd love to have a/nother child, but we can't afford one.' Economists have even been busy costing the raising of children. No precise sum has been arrived at, but most estimates involved tens of thousands of pounds.

Parents have always admonished children for their ingratitude, and have stressed the cost of feeding and clothing them. In poor societies, of course, children were an investment in a pair of hands and a safeguard for old age: that some would almost certainly die in infancy meant that to cover yourself you had to have several. But the idea of a child as a major item of consumption is a curious development, particularly if it is to be balanced carefully against a new car or a country cottage. Ancient myths portray children as the devourers of their parents, and there is a level on which this has always been true. But the transposition of myth into economic reality is another recent development in our advanced civilization. Our version of infancy devours not only the parents but also disproportionate quantities of the earth's resources. Is it because parents have some obscure sense that their own progeny are rivals in their shared dependency on the goods and services to which their needs – like the needs of adults – are articulated from the moment they first draw breath, that so many people hesitate before they bring into being another real infant in competition with the infantilized adults they have become? In this world parents become, less the bringers-up of children, than the providers of money to purchase the necessities for a safe passage through infancy – all those things so readily furnished by the emporia devoted to the creation of a world fit for children to inhabit. When shops are called Mothercare, what is there left for mothers to do, if not to buy?

Whatever vestigial deprivations parents impose upon themselves, the child must be spared, for its needs are sacred. If we want to understand why so many families break up, why fathers desert, and children are neglected and mistreated, is it not perhaps because of gathering resentment at the idealized world of happy childhood (which no parent could ever live up to), and rage at the greater urgency of the wants of children over those of adults? Many of us are simply too frail to balance this violent contradiction and reconcile it within ourselves. A culture which infantilizes its adults will find it difficult to do more than over-compensate with its real infants. Those images of children beaten, mutilated, abused, burnt with cigarettes, are produced at least as much by the workings of an economic system as by the wickedness of individual human nature. It sometimes seems that money has become the basic nutrient in the feeding of children's emotional and spiritual development. The inability of parents to care adequately for the children they love because of poverty and insufficiency is one thing; but how shall we describe the incapacitating power of money upon those of whom nothing is asked other than that they buy all that appears to be needed for their growth through time? No infant must ever wake up from its happy dreams, crying in the night, when the best that money can buy has been expended on allaying anxiety and dispelling the shadows, as well as extinguishing the curiosity that might be tempted to peer beyond the giant blue panda on the pillow, or the mobiles turning above the bed.

Of course all these goods, services and experiences are, in themselves, unexceptionable. The trouble is, they are not allowed to exist in themselves but must appear in the world reflecting an alien lustre which comes from the money which alone will secure them. When money and monetized transactions have become so dominant and pervasive, it is clear that we have left the realm of rational answers to human need, and have moved into that mysterious half-light of the soul where the stirrings of faith have their origin. Money has become the one sacrament, whereby access is gained to the beatific vision of capitalism's fullness. Money is the emancipator from the ordinariness of living. To be very rich is to be blessed: money is divine grace materialized. If only we buy the proper objects, the appropriate experiences, the necessary sensations, we shall transcend this mundane humanity, and know what it is to be truly happy. Lest we should doubt the efficacy of these symbols of transformation, the creative workings of a devoted advertising industry hold up before us an extensive iconography of transfiguration.

The indispensable commodities do not appear in the world in a vacuum. They also require a vast underpinning structure of expertise and of caring services. These are provided by the welfare state, which at the same time depends upon the continuing growth and expansion of the very processes which it is called upon to remedy. Thus the provision of technology to treat many symptoms of the endemic stress of our culture can be made only if that culture goes on in existing patterns of development. This, in turn, means not only creating more wealth but also, with it, deeper levels of stress and strain upon the human frame. We need more social workers and geriatric hospitals and cardiac units and emergency accident services and addiction programmes and detoxification centres, precisely because of the intensifying casualty rate in the war of all against all. The fact that the welfare state is the proudest ornament of those political groupings which see themselves as antagonistic towards capitalism in one of the great paradoxes of our time. What appeared as the triumph of human need over economic imperatives turns out to be, in fact, a symbiotic, even parasitic, relationship between them. In other words, money is the life-blood of the welfare state no less than the profit-making system on which it depends. (This is what leads Labour politicians to demand a 'cash-transfusion for the National Health Service which is haemorrhaging so badly'.) Indeed, the existence of the welfare state now depends upon faith in money and what it can buy, no less than the capitalist system itself. Far from being in opposition to the processes that grind up humanity, it is a means of servicing that dehumanizing machine. That an improved welfare state would be inconceivable without vast sums of money being pumped into it is a commonplace; and this is the limit of Labour's ambition. This is what the totalizing and all-embracing faith in money does to us. It renders the formulation of alternative forms of caring unthinkable. Alternatives are doomed to remain within the gravitational pull of the guiding star of capitalism, and may shine only in its reflected light.

It is not just reformist practices which have failed to emancipate us from the vital imperatives of capital; the very language in which the promises of socialism are expressed is now thin, debilitated. The reasons for this are complex and paradoxical. It will not have escaped even the most casual listener to the rhetoric of the Left that it draws heavily upon the imagery and vocabulary of religion. The socialist story is told in terms of the crusade, preaching socialism, making converts, spreading the word, preaching the message in and out of season. It refers to socialist vision, theology, dogma, holy writ, the tenets of the faith. It is a commonplace that the way to socialism will not be easy. So there is a need to fight the good fight, to avoid falling by the wayside in the many years that must be spent in the wilderness; there is the necessity of avoiding backsliding and of expelling doubters and apostates and heretics. All the evils of sectarianism beset the true (if broad) church. The faith must be lived, its purity maintained, there must be socialism by example. There remains always the hope of the Promised Land, the New Jerusalem, the socialist millennium, the day of the coming of the revolution, when the prophets will be vindicated and the socialist transformation begun. For in many versions of socialism, nothing less than the redemption of humanity is the eschatological teaching of the faith. The words which once had so much power in the mouths of those Methodists who had taken their faith with them into the trade unions, sound arid and empty now. They have become the daily currency of political journalists ('The party faithful were ready for a bit of socialist uplift', 'The militants, for whom Clause Four was the ark of the covenant', etc.).

Where has the substance gone from these fine phrases? Why don't they rouse echoes in hearts they are supposed to quicken? If these appear hollow clichés, it is because they are the husks of a faith that has withered. That this faith itself was derivative and often unacknowledged, gives added poignancy to these shells of belief, the fossilized bone-structure of the Labour Movement, fit now only for glass cases in the museums of labour history, or to be displayed in the recreated Socialist Sunday Schools of history workshops, like the relics of miracle-working saints. Faith itself never dies; though the faith which moves mountains can itself be moved.

The reason for this evacuation is clear. Faith based on the gospel of work has also deserted its traditional capitalist temples – the mills and manufactories, the palaces of production – and taken up its abode in new, more diffused places of worship: the shopping precincts and enclosures, the palaces of display. In consequence, not only are the traditional church buildings – the sites of worship and work both – empty and derelict, turned over to warehouses or depositories or car-parks, but those socialist shrines, constructed at least partly in their sacred image, are even more abandoned, overgrown with weeds, indeed almost effaced.

10

No faith which commands and expresses the hope of the people is proof against decay, no matter how strongly institutionalized and socially rooted it may appear to have become. Why should it surprise us if the Labour Party should be passing through these same processes of dissolution and attenuation? After all, there are many examples of other sects, faiths and religions which have carried, however briefly, the hopes and longings of oppressed peoples. Anthropology is rich in records of people whose deepest certainties have been informed with the hope of millenarian deliverance, hopes which have also given them the courage to resist oppression, and at the same time to sustain alternative ways of being in the world in their everyday lives. Think of the ghost-dance religion of the North American Indians, who believed that their dance would summon the hosts of their own dead to fight alongside them in their struggle to rid their land of the white invaders, and to reinstate their own traditions of harmony and balance. Imagine the millenarian fantasies of the English poor, suffering the incomprehensible dislocations of the early industrial era – for instance the adherents of the prophetess Joanna Southcott, with her promise that she would bear the deliverer, and whose box of sealed writings were to be opened at the appointed hour. Nor is our time exempt from the fervours of chiliastic expectation: those to whom other forms of hope are denied readily find a place in the congregations who look forward to that new dispensation which will depose the mighty and exalt the humble after the Second Coming.

It may be that the fate of the Labour Party (with which so many failing hopes and expectations are still so deeply implicated) can be illuminated by the history of minor and more marginal sects once devoted to similar, if more overtly religious, dreams of transformation. The origins, the rise and flourishing, and finally the decay of such sects can be comprehensively traced, often rooted in the despair of the rural poor of early industrial Britain. Though many of these sects long predated the Labour Party, the echoes of their hymns can still be heard, if faintly, today. Such a group was the Cokelers, who were active on the Surrey–Sussex border in the middle of the last century. Today, the few remaining Cokelers meet in their chapel of the Society of the Dependents. Built in the 1960s, it has a gabled front in red and silver brick and a circular window, now painted over. Inside, the walls are whitewashed; sash windows and hard modern pews, a thin strip of crimson cushion on the seats. A length of carpet runs along the aisle, and the wood-block floor smells of new polish. The elders sit on a platform behind a modern desk, with a crimson velvet curtain against the wooden partition which separates the disused half of the chapel. At 10.20 on a Sunday morning, there are eight or nine people present, the youngest of them in her sixties: elderly women for the most part, in shiny straw summer hats. Most have a coat or a cardigan folded behind them to protect their backs from the hard upright wood. The dark red hassocks are unused: most of the people are too old to kneel. On the desk is a big black Bible. A gleam of June sunlight strikes its gold edges as the pages are turned. All who will attend are there some minutes before the meeting begins; an intense, reflective silence becomes almost tangible in the still morning.

The meeting is informal. An improvised prayer is followed by an unaccompanied hymn written by John Sirgood, who founded the sect in the 1850s, which was given the unflattering name of 'Cokelers' by the local people, from their preference for drinking cocoa when they met in each other's houses. 'We are called Dependents', said one old woman. 'People often say "Don't you mean Independent?" But we depend solely on the grace and goodness of God.' John Sirgood arrived in Loxwood with his wife and a handcart, fleeing, it is said, the smallpox. Originally a shoemaker in Gloucestershire, he became a member of the South Essex 'Peculiar People', before moving to Loxwood, where the group could pursue its own form of worship and belief. The survival of the Cokelers has been due partly to their millenarian faith, their rejection of the world, the persecution of the early years, and also to their strong network of support and mutual help. They sing

> Their enemies are all confused
> Who greatly tried to do them harm.

The elder who conducts the meeting talks for half an hour, a mixture of homely images and Biblical expressions: many Cokelers read no secular books. His text is from the first chapter of Paul's Epistle to the Corinthians: the wisdom and learning of the world are as nothing to the wisdom of the heart that knows God. Because most of the members of the sect were farm servants, labourers and small farmers, and were persecuted by those they disturbed with the sometimes noisy fervours of their meetings, there remains a faint distrust of learning, and an insistence on the 'powers' given to the humble. In spite of this, many people did learn to read and write through the chapel. 'There was an old shepherd who only had five days' schooling in his life. He was always a bit slow reading his Bible, but everybody was very patient because he'd been taught to read by the elders.'

The theme of the morning is that Christ is within us: the darkness, the desolation, the wilderness of the outer world against the light and joy within. Life is a pilgrimage, from which we do not know when we shall awake to the promise – our hope, our sure hope – that has been given us.

When he has finished, those who feel moved to testify rise to their feet. In their voices are the cadences and inflexions of the old country accent, informed with the spirit of long-dead parents and friends. They speak of the time when the chapels were so full that people gathered in the chapel yard with the windows wide open so that they could hear what was said. They evoke a multitude of believers, whose absence is not mourned, because they live in daily expectation of seeing them again: George Cuff, an illitcrate carter, on his knees in the stable at the end of each day's work, when the words of praise flowed from his lips; Brother Roland, 'a soldier in Queen Victoria's army. He said they had always to be ready for the bugle-call. They didn't know when it would come, but they had always to be expecting it, with their puttees and their tunic ready. And so it is with us: the call can come at any time, and we must be ready.'

The faith, once so exuberantly expressed, is more inturned now. The archaic and decorous phrases refer to the indwelling spirit, the light vouchsafed for us, the certainty of the near end of all things. Some of the more particular observances have fallen away, and the millennial sense of poor and oppressed people has been muted with their Antinomian belief that those reborn in their faith could be without sin. But the frugality of their life remains, the plain living of people who were expected to eschew ornament in their homes, and even flowers. Celibacy was celebrated by them, for it permitted a closer relationship with God. They relied on conversion to increase their numbers, and many of those present came to the Dependents in that way.

The stories of persecution live on, and John Sirgood's memory evokes memories of miraculous happenings. 'A crowd was waiting for him one day outside the meeting house. They carried sticks and stones, and were so angry, I think they would have killed him.

But they waited and waited in vain. He passed among them unseen.' In the early days, people were turned out of their homes and jobs for belonging to the sect. 'They've had their few sticks of furniture put out on the street, but there has always been one of the brethren to take them in. They have been pelted with eggs and stones. A magistrate once tried to fine them £10; but the law against conventicles had been repealed and he couldn't do it. A boy called Eli Errington came to the chapel one Sunday morning with a group of lads. They were all wearing their jackets inside out as a sign of disrespect. But such was John Sirgood's power and truth that Eli went outside and turned his jacket round. He stayed and became one of our staunchest members. They learned endurance you see.'

The apartness of their lives led the Cokelers to create a strong structure of mutual help and support. They spread to many neighbouring villages, and built chapels as far away as Chichester, Hove and South Norwood. They built co-operative shops in the villages, in which they came as close to self-reliance as possible. The Combination Stores still stand in Loxwood, with their red shingled roof and dusty windows, now empty and awaiting demolition. The stores provided work and accommodation for those who had lost their jobs and homes. There were bakehouses, food-stores and workshops, all run on strictly co-operative lines. 'At one time, there were twenty-two people sat down to meals round the table at Warnham. They used to tend each other in sickness, lay each other out when they died. They did everything that merciful and loving hands could do, and that is a great deal. Of course, the old persecution died out. There's tolerance today, but it is the tolerance of indifference. I'm not sure that is so much better.'

The Cokelers grew to their maximum number – about 2,000 – in 1885, the year of Sirgood's death. 'My mother used to tell me about his funeral. They came from all the other chapels, the biggest meeting there had ever been. Of course, my great-uncle remembered the chapel being built. They put their pence together and built it themselves. That was in 1861.'

The old exaltation may have gone, but there remains a directness and a simplicity in the testimony of the people, a manner that suggests an older country sensibility that has now almost completely disappeared. When they express their pleasure at the bright June day and its birdsong, and they give thanks that they have been spared another week to meet together again, they mean it. That they had freely received from God and must give freely to others in return underlay their social practice. Many older people in the village remember the neighbourliness and charity of the Cokelers. 'They were good people, I wish we had them back again', was a common reaction in the area, even in the mid 1980s. Even those whose attitude was one of amused scepticism towards their beliefs insisted on their goodness. One old man in his seventies said 'I used to go with my Aunt Kate every Sunday morning while my mother was dying of cancer. I was about nine. I remember how I was never allowed a second piece of bread and butter because they needed the coupons for her Benger's Food. They were kind to me at the chapel. But they did used to rant. One man used to get up and shout "There was a man who built his house on top of a hill. And there came a great wind that blew and blew; and the roof fell in and the walls fell down; but he was not harmed. He was saved because he was one who had faith."'

The Cokelers were pacifist. In the First World War they sent a letter to Asquith, saying that it was impossible that their young men should become soldiers, and pleading that conscientious objectors should be freed from military service. 'Of course, at the time, they were mostly Liberals. I dare say that by now some of them have become Conservative, but I'm not. At the time they used to upset a lot of people. The old brethren were perhaps a little too austere. There was no drinking or smoking. I never saw any of them wear a brooch, much less an earring; no paint on their face. No ornament, no pictures in the house. We never went to picture galleries, and theatres were unheard-of. Our lives might have been narrow, but they ran deep; and we learned wisdom. I feel sorry for young people now; they know so little. People have said to me "But what about enjoying yourself while you're young?" But they don't know the joy that is within us, within all of us. We wanted nothing, because it was all in the heart and the spirit. Being together, fellowship, the help we gave each other – what could be more joyful than that? And the yearly meeting at the mother-church here in Loxwood, how can I describe it? They'd bring their own food, and come and stay for three days. The church would be so full, they'd have benches down the aisles. All the women would be wearing their poke bonnets trimmed with blue or black velvet. Very becoming they were too. But for the rest of the time they were plain-living, hard-working people. When my great-aunt was a girl, she was up at four in the morning, milking cows. If they were ill, they used to wait for deliverances – that was a kind of faith-healing, because of course they could never afford to pay doctors' bills. But we always knew that the end of all things was close; and then the world would become like the Garden of Eden again:

> A King in righteousness shall reign
> And rule the earth in peace,
> When desolations have an end
> And wars and tumults cease;
> When all creation shall be saved
> From suffering and from pain,
> And earth itself shall be restored,
> Like Eden bloom again.

'People used to speak with such passion and power. We never believed in the bread and wine, because Jesus told us that He is within us already. The outpouring of the Holy Spirit at Pentecost meant that He is dwelling inside us. We did not need the bread and the wine.'

I I

The debates about the 'credibility of socialism' are the palest acknowledgement of the multiple mutations that faith has undergone. While socialists have raged at religion as a form of social control, at its contribution to the false consciousness of the people, they have often been about the business of constructing a false consciousness of their own. While denying the need for faith, they have at the same time urged it upon, and required it from, their own flock. Capitalism has demonstrated the falseness of socialism's alternative faith (or false consciousness). This it has done by swallowing up the energies which were once restricted to the sacred space, and spewing them forth in its own secular version of the word made flesh. The transcendence that religion once offered, often in an afterlife (or in moments of *ekstasis* in this life), is now to be sought in the here and now, and money is its sole sacrament. To say that the hope of transcendence has deserted the churches and is now celebrated only in the market-place is not simply a metaphor: it is as close as you can get to describing the numinosity which emanates from market transactions. If capitalism no longer needs to promise the eternal feasting of the blest, is it not because its own everyday banquets have a celestial savour, are penetrated by a spiritual aroma, which rises up like incense from the precincts and enclosures where money changes hands, and much more besides?

The Victoria Centre in Nottingham. What is most striking is the silence of the crowds. You can hear a mildly euphoric music above the shuffling feet on the marble causeways, and the splashing of a great coloured cascade in the middle of the ground floor. The space is like the nave of a cathedral; the shop fronts are stained-glass windows, full of stylized models in expressionist poses.

The place is a permanent exhibition, part *kermis*, part communion. Here, all human pleasures and aspirations have been captured and priced. The display combines the search for happiness with a sense of the great public rituals that have decayed. The names of products – Jupiter, Saturn, Aztec, Odyssey, Vivaldi, Windsor, Savannah, Olympic, Capri, Imperial – represent a cosmic ransacking of time and place, to describe beds, duvets, fashion valances, chairs, dining tables, digital clocks; a piracy that creates an impression of effortless mobility and power. Revolutions and miracles are advertised in the preparation of dessert foods and the washing of underwear; and in this way, politics and religion are put in their place.

Things are full of promise; not only of well-being and comfort, but even of immortality. Siliconized polypropylene, "no deterioration", "there for ever". You are invited to sleep on a white cloud filled with soft Dacron, serenity Latex foam, four-poster beds, a home solarium, interior log saunas, marble caskets for bathing, water massage in sealed cabinets like up-ended coffins. Leisure and escape are everywhere; relaxation and sleep. Everything is caressing and somniferous. This place proposes a world which manages to combine the beatific vision with the occupational therapy workshop; it is the kind of setting in which my grandmother might have hoped she would spend eternity.

Not only has capitalism incarnated for us the celestial paradise, suffused with the angelic music of the spheres, but it has also been able to give corporeal shape to those socialist promises which 'actually existing socialism' has so clearly failed to redeem. The topography of contemporary capitalism in the rich countries is reminiscent of nothing so much as the dreams of the early socialist visionaries, dreams which at the time capitalism dismissed as hopelessly utopian. Such visions, they were then told, could never be expected to materialize in this vale of tears, but could be only the fitting reward when we were called to our heavenly home. Conversely, existing socialism, in the Soviet Union for instance, has been at pains to dispel dreams of heaven while at the same time proclaiming the secular miracles it has wrought. Such miracles leave its young population gazing towards the colourful iconography of the materialized dreams of the West (for what else is it they are seeking when they surreptitiously approach Western visitors, offering extravagant handfuls of roubles for a pair of blue jeans, which apparently possess an aura denied to the merely functional domestic equivalent?), while its older citizens fill the churches. Western societies have, it seems, ingested the promises of socialism, and reproduced a simulacrum of them, whilst taunting those societies which have clung to the revealed formulations of socialism with their inability to yield what they promised, or even to match capitalism's version of what was socialism's original dream.

If capitalism has been so successful that it has been able to triumph over the opposition, both sacred and secular, ancient and modern, who can but marvel and admire? How fortunate we are to be living in so triumphant a dispensation; to be on what appears the winning side of history. The ability of capitalism to commoditize and extract profit from both religion and anti-religious socialism should make us hesitate before pronouncing yet again upon its imminent collapse and terminal crisis. Marx's paean of praise to the resourcefulness and energy of capitalism, which has struck so many readers of the *Communist Manifesto*, has proved, for all its magniloquence, a poor and inadequate estimate of its protean possibilities.

Of course there is a flaw, as in all grand designs, or indeed accidents, if that is what capitalism is. In these vast reworkings of ideology and faith, which individuals embrace as personal belief, it is human beings who pay the price, increasingly locked, as they are, into a system which is both totalitarian and deforming. Western society is totalitarian because it can allow no genuine alternatives to exist on its own terrain, but must absorb them and recreate them in its own image. Its pluralism, its variety, its celebrated freedom of choice, operate only in the universe it has created. Who would wish to flee from this paradise? What serpent could lure us to eat of the fruit of the tree of knowledge in this garden of earthly delights, after which our eyes might be opened, so that we would see both each other's, and our own, nakedness and vulnerability? Perhaps as an added precaution, our current faith proclaims the fruit of this tree to be both unappetizing and impossible to digest.

Western society is deforming because it constantly reworks and counterfeits human needs and desires in forms from which it can make monetary gain. Every liberatory impulse, whether it be religious or socialist, must be captured and transformed into what the system can sell. This means that the deepest yearnings and profoundest aspirations sometimes assume the most bizarre, indeed, barely recognizable shapes, both material and immaterial. Some of the simplest activities and experiences have to carry a charge and bear a freight of meaning which is actually inappropriate, and bears witness to felt absences elsewhere. Nothing leaves us to the innocent enjoyment of what it is, but catches us up in exaltations and excitements which belong in other realms, and which must stand in place of other forms of transcendence which our culture cannot permit, indeed spares no one and nothing in suppressing.

This does not necessarily mean that the system always succeeds in falsifying our generous impulses. For all its power capitalism is never, and can never be, totally or finally successful. Indeed, not only do people constantly find occasions for mutuality and altruism, for celebrating the gift of being alive, but they also use the products and materialities of capitalism in ways that run counter to the imperatives of the system – indeed defy and subvert it. However, we cannot escape the dilemma that these very objects used to express our generosity and our caring for each other are implicated, however remotely and obscurely, in a death-dealing system. What shall we say of the meal prepared by loving hands out of courgettes flown from Ethiopia at the time of the famine? Or of the congratulatory bouquet of carnations grown on land in South America which once sustained in food many people who also loved one another? Joyfulness, pleasure, delight are real enough, no matter in what social or economic order they express themselves; to what extent these are altered when they are won at the expense of the sorrowing, pain or misery of others (however remote), there exists at present no measure to gauge.

12

The politics of hope have become choked with the debris of the myths (or faiths) that have crumbled. That the politics of hope are based upon myths is not the problem; indeed, all great political movements are based upon myth. That these myths must be taken for truth in order to lead to action always has ambiguous, and sometimes disastrous, consequences for the lives of women and men in the world. For it is difficult to imagine modest myths. They are by nature epic, grandiose, all-compelling, and once set in train, they have a life of their own and follow rules which are not of our making. The great contemporary myths of race and class have littered the world with human bones, as indeed have at one time or another all the great world religions.

The socialist version of the politics of hope has always depended, however distantly, upon the great heroic story of a redemptive proletariat. Whatever energy and encouragement the myth has provided to sustain people in their struggle against injustice and exploitation, it has proved in the end to be deeply disabling, both in those places like the Soviet Union, where it has been the source of a stifling and incapacitating orthodoxy; and in the Western countries, where it has diverted the parties of the Left from paying atention to what has actually been happening in the lives of the people. If the heroic content of the story has decayed in the West, this is not due simply to any inadequacy that the myth itself might have, but is in part a result of the changed world situation, in which a largely black proletariat in the countries of the South faces a principally white *petite bourgeoisie* in the countries of the North, a *petite bourgeoisie* which now includes great numbers of those who formerly constituted the national working classes. Thus, although the myth may still be able to galvanize and sustain many struggles in the Third World, the myth of the proletariat serves now only to distance those Western workers who have enjoyed improvements in their living conditions at the expense of those workers who are poor, black and remote from them in space. Although that myth may still have human, living content in Nicaragua, South Africa or the Phillipines, it is already doubly disfigured and invaded everywhere, both by the patterns of development in the West which have marginalized it here, and equally by its distorted embodiment in the bureaucratized inflexibilities of the socialism of Eastern Europe.

The myth of the working class depended essentially upon the concept of suffering through labour, which would render people more and more poor, a suffering that could be ended only by an act of rebellion, and the consequent transformation of the oppressive values of society. However, the rich capitalist societies have succeeded in large measure in removing the forms of primary suffering on which that redemptive project was grounded. This is not to say that the Western working class no longer suffers. What is true is that the forms of the suffering have changed. The sufferings inflicted by labour have been alleviated, both by intensive mechanization and robotization on the one hand, and by the transfer of the labour which induced it to other parts of the world. This is experienced by the Western working class as a blessed relief from older impositions. Into this free space, which is served by a labour not abolished but merely exported, pour all kinds of other evils and wrongs and forms of suffering, some of which were scarcely known to those earlier toilers in field and factory. Who can doubt, looking at Western society, that it seethes with an afflicted humanity, assailed by loneliness, a sense of meaninglessness, a lack of function and purpose, a search for the consolations

of escape, through drugs, violence, alcohol, the sicknesses of
self-indulgence, through any form of escape from the self? These
penalties are seen as an acceptable price for the release from
earlier forms of poverty and labour. Such barbarities should not
be seen as acceptable, for they damage and destroy people no less
than those earlier horrors which are now the object of historical
curiosity in the West, but daily experience in the Third World.
These avoidable visitations of late-twentieth-century capitalism
can be revealed as the abominations they are only by means of an
alternative myth, of some other story than that of a working class
which, once in power, would bring harmony to the world.

Why do people seem so slow to dispel the shadows that darken
their enjoyment of the capitalist goods? The only way in which
these afflictions are rendered tolerable is, of course, by their
undoubted association with all the benefits which capitalism has
bestowed upon the people. We fear that if we attempt to attack the
evils, we may at the same time abolish the goods. Thus an
equilibrium of terror is set up, whereby progress means economic
growth for us, no matter what barbarities attend it in our experience, and no matter what privations it passes on to the world's
poor. Here is the clue to the quiescence, the passivity, the
apparent apathy, the indifference of the people of the West. Here
also, a key to the causes of the violence, the sense of impotence,
the suppressed rage, the cruelty – to so many of the feelings which
we ourselves have expressed: for these feelings are clearly not
confined to the marginalized and the non-conforming, but run wide
and deep. The fact that they appear in people's personal lives, and
not in political discourse, is the price exacted in the bargain struck
by capitalism with the people, on its own terms. Any politics which
do not address this immobilism and unspoken fear, have forfeited
the right to call themselves radical. Those who declare that the key
to the council-house door, or the rising curve of disposable
income, are sufficient to assuage all anguish, and mark the

extreme limits of human possibilities, have not realized the true nature of the Faustian pact between capital and labour in the West, with its only briefly postponed day of reckoning.

The impotence of the once-powerful myth of the working class could not be more plain in this context. The denial of this obvious fact by the Labour Left, and the conclusion of Labour's alleged realists that the mythic days are past, and what we must concentrate on is making the system work more efficiently, together combine to prolong the wintry immobilism in which our political life is frozen. All we are told is that we must be optimistic. We must keep faith. We must look to the future and not continue to fight the battles of the past. In other words, taboos and proscriptions are erected to hide the empty places where the myths once lived. The deep source of the potency of Conservatism in the 1980s is that it not only saw the need for myth – however tawdry, second-hand and vulgar this may have been – but it also perceived how little lay behind the heroic façades of the Left:

> GLENDOWER: I can call spirits from the vasty deep.
> HOTSPUR: Why so can I, or so can any man,
> But will they come when you do call for them?

Such was the riposte to Labour's posturing.

The renewal of political life in Britain demands the recreation, or perhaps the discovery, of myth. Of course, this is a dangerous project, not least because all myths seek to transcend themselves and propose themselves to the people as truth. That is to say, all myth – and not only its capitalist version – has a totalizing impulse, which invites, indeed requires, out-groups of disbelievers who, for their own sake, must be coerced into recognizing the truth. Myth is also dangerous because it draws upon unconscious energies, which have their own dynamic development and mode of making their way in the world. It is probably the case that they cannot be artificially created, though it is certainly true that they lend themselves to elaboration and extension. For instance, there was no need for the British sense of racial superiority in the assembling of their empire to be codified or set out in any text; it was, as it were, innate and self-evident. Christopher Hibbert, describing the so-called Indian Mutiny of 1857, describes how these sentiments became more explicit under the impetus of the uprising:

Letters written by officers to their families were full of the most lurid details of rapes and violations and of what Lieutenant Arthur Moffat Lang called 'perpetual lying reports about massacres in churches and other places.' Major Baillie reported to his father that English ladies had been sold by auction in the bazaars; that children had been roasted alive before the eyes of their mothers down whose throats bits of the flesh were forced, before they, too, were killed. George Blake said that an officer who fell into enemy hands had a finger and toe cut off every day. Kendall Goghill told his family that at Meerut an officer's wife had been dragged from church, stripped and her breasts cut off. At Delhi, ladies had been publicly dishonoured in the streets before being massacred . . .
Believing these myths the rage of British officers and civilian officials knew no bounds. Garnet Wolseley looked forward to the wholesale destruction of the 'black-faced curs' who had been guilty of such dastardly crimes. Dr Wise hoped that a bloody revenge would be taken. 'An awful example must be made', he wrote. 'No mercy shown to any prisoners. Death to all who have arms. When this crisis is over, the Hindu must be treated as a servant and kept in his place, not treated and supported as a pampered dependant.'

Nazism shows most clearly how the power of myth may be abused, and the work of Nazi intellectuals demonstrates how easy it was to make use of quite sophisticated anthropological studies in the service of their ghoulish myth. Some might consider the development of Marxism – that myth which claims to be a science – particularly in the academies of the West, to represent the ultimate refinement of mythic hermeneutics.

Myths cannot be summoned; indeed, they summon us. It is our subservience to them that makes them so seductive and so treacherous. However, without them, life has no meaning, or at least no meaning that can move the heart. In the West, capitalism is clearly the dominant mythic structure. Those who would have us believe that we live by reason, all who would represent the West as the triumph of rationality, are profoundly in error. Yet again, myth has played its finest hand. We are installed at the centre of the myth which informs our whole lives, and of course, we do not perceive it as such. It is all the easier not to see the mythic structure we inhabit, because it has become the dominant configuration of the world. The myth of capital indeed has a lot going for it. Its strength and power are almost without precedent; but we shouldn't, for all that, mistake it for truth, even though it continues to make daily converts in what used to be considered the remotest corners of the earth.

PART THREE
Futures

13

Because capitalism has eaten up and absorbed into itself religious modes of experience and forms of belief, and now appears in the world as a material religion (in the sense that within its own materialities it appears to make spiritual transcendence available), it is necessary that any alternative political philosophy which sets out to challenge capitalism at a fundamental level, must obtain for itself a similar potency and mythic dimension. One religion can be successfully overthrown only by another. This new gospel must be one whose truths appear to offer liberation from oppression, fear and bondage.

While capitalism still seems to retain its command over many of the faithful, the sacrifices it demands of the earth and its people are in our time becoming insupportable. Even were it a religion that offered the most refined and profound spiritual solace to a suffering humanity, its continued supremacy would still be in jeopardy. As it is, not only do its most committed votaries find their lives haunted by dissatisfactions and emptinesses and obsessive cravings which it has no power to exorcize or to vanquish, but its victims frequently yield the tribute of their lives through malnutrition, avoidable disease and excess of labour. And in this process, the whole earth is being transformed into a site of desolation that threatens to become unfit for mere habitation. Unlike more modest slum clearances which sought to improve the ravages caused by earlier capitalist projects, it is hard to imagine where the inhabitants of the earth will be evacuated to whilst their world is repaired. The more eager and far-sighted apologists of the faith would no doubt see us transported to distant colonies in space, leaving the earth as a gigantic kind of inner city, left to the predations of who knows what, where it can burn itself out harmlessly, whilst we view the spectacle from the comfort of our paradises regained, succumbing only to the odd twinge of nostalgia for the neighbourhood we had to leave behind.

Myths, of course, cannot be invented, at least not those which have the power to draw upon the deepest energies of the human spirit. We should seek, therefore, to animate an adequate countervailing myth which has the potential to subvert the capitalist faith, and which already exists in the world. This is no longer, however much it may once have appeared to be, the old-time religion of scientific socialism. Rather it is the myth of the planet – a planet menaced by a human hubris which has long grown insensitive to the relationship between human beings and the natural base which sustains them – which grows more and more potent. Nature, which was assumed to be a mere backcloth, enduring for ever and ever, against which human destiny would play itself out until the end of time (or the Day of Judgement to those of more archaic religious sensibilities), turns out to be vulnerable and limited, a most delicate organism, and one which, moreover, is doubly subject to destruction at our hands, whether cataclysmically through nuclear war, or by stealth, through its erosion and exhaustion by our daily relationship with it.

This everyday relationship of exploitation is embodied in economic systems which claim to be the reflection on earth of natural law. What more profane or distorted travesty of our relationship with living nature and of the needs of the human spirit could possibly have been conjured up by the most disordered imagination, and then installed and elaborated in the realm of reason? Thus the immutable laws of political economy, which have been reasserted with such vigour and ebullience in our time, are constructed upon a more than mutable foundation, which is the perishable and wasting body of the natural world. Whether the 'laws' of political economy are based upon a lie about how human beings unalterably relate to each other is debatable; what is no longer in question, except by the high priests of orthodox economics (and hence by their trusting congregations), is that the deep assumptions on which existing economic practice is based, will ruin us all, if they are not opposed by even more compelling beliefs.

The alternative myth which many people are discovering is, above all, about changes in relationships. It is almost as if the condition of the earth, with its scars and mutilations, has become a parable for the way we have treated each other. To be more precise, it has become an objective correlative of what the capitalist system has done to people who live under its dominion: having gutted, exhausted and used up their human substance, it has discarded them. Those who would persuade us that the only hope for humankind is to continue in the ways that have become familiar in the last two hundred years could not be more misleading prophets.

The green myth has the undoubted advantage of appearing to be true; and that is the primary requirement for an informing belief, which lies at the base of any religious work. It is not given to us to know whether this contestatory myth is at some metaphysical level truer or less true than the religion it opposes. It is sufficient for us, living in this world as we must, that it makes a future possible, and gives back hope of a life to come – though not in a secular hereafter which is dependent upon the continuing observance of the sacred laws of political economy, nor in any other afterlife than that which pledges continuity with those living here and now.

Of course, all myths must appear true, and must offer the promise of liberation. Even capitalism, when it made its 'bloody appearance in the world', appeared to have great liberatory potential. Did it not promise to abolish poverty, and to free human beings from the oppressive social relations which feudalism had imposed? The problem of any myth is that in order to move people to act in the world, and to offer itself as a possible vehicle for the realization of human aspirations, it must claim a truth that is absolute, and thereby become a religion. Capitalism as a world religion has increasingly subordinated people to its version of revelation, with conspicuously greater success, it has to be said, than those forms of socialism which have cherished a similar ambition.

The green myth, at present considered a primitive cult fit only for utopians, and other peripherals and simple-minded folk, is actually deeply radicalizing, vibrant with emancipatory promise. Because it is still in the process of becoming, remains mobile and embryonic, there is at this time no danger of its taking on those oppressive aspects which more established myths exhibit. However, this does not mean that it will remain for all time proof against such temptations. Nothing could be more damaging than that it should be contaminated and deformed by those capitalist structures in which it must, of necessity, make its first appearance. The fate of reformist socialism in the West offers the cruellest warning and example. Thus, under any capitalist take-over of the green myth, some of the ugliest scenarios might be played out. For instance, the idea of a lack of resources easily translates into a concern with overpopulation: and the Malthusian tradition is always available to be drawn upon for answers. In such a context, mass starvation becomes a regrettable necessity for those for whom there is no place laid at nature's banquet. Capitalism's sublime indifference to merely human purposes would readily exploit the green myth, and in the process exterminate whole populations in the superior interest of concealing the fact that it is the rich of the earth who are the source and origin of all waste and abuse of finite resources. Sacrifice is a key element in all religions, but we must beware of the nature of the sacrifice that might be exacted by any marriage of convenience between capitalism and the green myth, on the terms of 'actually existing capitalism'. More than this: just as capitalism's increments throughout its long history of growth have been unequally distributed, so it may well be that its necessary retrenchments, under the guise of limited resources, might be distributed in a similarly skewed ratio. Thus the poor might become very poor indeed, while the rich remain agreeably cushioned against want; and all in the name of 'conservation'. Those who accuse the Greens of caring more for nature than for humanity misunderstand that environmental ruin is both a reflection and consequence of how we abuse and exploit each other across the world.

Even if the green myth were to be so successful as actually to extinguish the old religion (apart from a few harmless sectarians singing the old choruses in decrepit conventicles) in the most benign of mass conversions, it would, no doubt, in its very moment of triumph, be in danger of hardening into dogma, or taking upon itself the more pernicious aspects of all revealed religions. For all myths tend to polarize the world between good and evil, and to separate out those who remain in the truth from those who obstinately cling to other, lesser creeds. Self-righteousness is sufficiently in evidence in the most self-critical minority cults for us to wonder what forms it might take were these minority faiths to become the prevailing orthodoxies.

At the individual level, what myths and religions primarily offer is a vision of unity, a sense of wholeness, a feeling of reconciliation between the individual and the universe, between the one and the many. This vision, by striking deep roots into the sources of the individual's psychic energies, activates the changes and transformations which make possible the living out of the new faith. In the case of the green myth also, unless there is an adequate understanding of, or accommodation with, the idea of evil, there is always the possibility that this unacknowledged evil will be projected onto others; and what more likely objects of such feeling than the non-believers, or even the faint-hearts? And before we claim a future superiority for the green myth, it has to be asked which religions have ever had such understanding of the place of evil in the world that they were able to resist killing? The sacrifice which a less destructive myth would require should be contained within the life of the individual. For myth speaks of the eternal, although it can be articulated only in time. This unavoidable contradiction must be recognized. The green myth is perhaps more modest in that it lends itself to no complete syntheses, no final resolutions.

It does however have deep continuities with earlier attempts to transform society. It is of a piece with the socialist hopes which sought to assure a decent and dignified sufficiency for all. Socialism sought to remove from people the daily anxieties and restrictions which came from not having enough to eat, from living in shelter dependent upon the whims of landlords, from oppressive and meaningless work. Above all, it aimed to reconstruct society so that our public life might cherish the same virtues as our private lives. It refused the lie that greed and competitiveness and taking advantage of the needs and weaknesses of others (all those things that would be abhorrent in the personal moral sphere) could become mysteriously transmuted into the most basic virtues of our social existence. Socialism sought to install human purposes and generous feelings at the centre of economic and social intercourse. It endeavoured to draw upon a universal insight into the common nature of human dereliction in the universe (we all die alone), and to mitigate unavoidable shared sufferings.

This same spirit informs the philosophy of the greens. Although it may appear more difficult to attain at this moment, this is nevertheless the appropriate reformulation of the socialist myth at this particular stage in the development of capitalism. It is particularly appropriate, because the way in which the international capitalist system has become increasingly unified, demands a response that is equally global. The idea of 'socialism in Britain' has a strangely archaic sound in a world from whose universal traffickings in money, commodities and people it cannot unilaterally extricate itself. That the Labour Left is pathologically unable to draw any effective conclusions (other than ritual intonations to internationalism) from this awesome reality, is what drains their critique of vitality and plausibility. Conversely, Labour's Right, which would have us recognize these necessities as the given bounds of all political discourse, gains in realism and a sense of inevitability because it has calculated that people, faced with the overwhelming difficulties that significant changes would entail, will turn away and be content with their individual preoccupations. The green myth excites and gives hope, both because it guides us towards familiar if neglected paths, and also gives fresh urgency to the need for curbing and redirecting those destructive forces which prevent us, as always, from living fully human lives, and now, refinement of horror, may prevent us from leading any lives at all.

The enabling energies set free by the green myth are the most liberating since those unleashed by the great myth developed by Marx. Indeed, there are clear parallels between them. Both myths are grounded in baleful historical processes run out of control, processes which are destructive of human beings, and which, if not transformed, will result in our common ruin, whether this be of the contending classes or of the species itself. Marx foresaw the destruction of the capitalist system. The greens foresee not only the destruction of this system, but of the very base which sustains and makes possible this or any other.

One of the greatest stengths of the Marxist myth was that it postulated an agency by whose intervention the transformation could be achieved. The greens can call upon no such great socio-economic formation as a proletariat (although, of course, their appeal is as much to the working class as to any other), but must needs rely upon humanity in general – a wider, but more nebulous category. Rudolf Bahro expresses it thus:

A striking fact of the present situation seems rather to be the unambiguous *dominance of the external contradictions of bourgeois society over its internal contradictions.* The East-West and especially the North–South contradictions prevail. The internal class struggle over real wages, over working and living conditions, shows the tendency to become a subordinate function of bourgeois society in its confrontation with the Second, Third and Fourth Worlds, and it is here that both national and international destiny will be determined, far more than by the play of internal conflicts.

In conditions such as these, it would be anachronistic and dangerous to continue striving for solutions via an intensification of the internal class contradictions. The question is rather to bring these into relative adjustment, in such a way that at the same time an external adjustment becomes possible in the form of a radically changed world economic order.

The greens are stronger in the demonstrable evidence of the ruinous consequences of the system they oppose, even though they are weaker in that the oppressions and violences do not have the same immediate subjective resonance (at least for the majority of the population in the rich world: in the countries of the South, it is different) as the sombre prophecies of deepening immiseration for the Western working class which Marx set forth. The green myth offers a possibility of transcending the immobilism which comes from the hitherto unnameable development of capitalism at the approach of the millennium (and chiliastic terminology seems oddly appropriate at this time). That is to say, the polarization which Marx anticipated within capitalist society has in fact been transferred onto a world scale. It is now largely true to see the North–South confrontation as being that of a principally white bourgeoisie in the North facing a predominantly black proletariat in the South. For those who think only within the classical categories of socialist revolution, this leaves scant prospect of a political project in the 'metropolitan' countries, and they therefore turn anxiously towards surrogate or quasi-proletariats at home in order to eke out their depleted ranks. Hence the call to minorities, the desperate search for alliances that will muster at least a shadow of the armies which have long since been demobilized from the sporadic skirmishings of an exhausted class war.

The leaden and lustreless impotence which follows from these unacknowledged developments, and which appears inexplicable to those on the Left still exhorting us to heroic acts of optimism, is capable of being dissolved as the green myth takes shape and grows. It is no longer a question of the poor of the earth imitating existing models of being rich. Nor yet does it involve the rich becoming dispossessed after the fashion of the existing poor. A joint action of both is indispensable, for their common home is threatened. For the rich this does mean a renunciation of familiar ways of living. It need not be an impoverishment (except in the most narrow sense), although it will no doubt be represented as such by those devoted to the maintenance of existing structures of power and wealth. A sacrifice is called for, but it is a sacrifice in the true meaning of the word – the giving up of a lesser good for a greater; and what could be a greater good than survival? We must assume that the rich love their children more than they love their wealth, and that they see in them future prospects other than the enjoyment of fortunes their parents have amassed. We take this to be true, for we have seen that the poor make every effort to avoid their children having to inherit the poverty that has been their lot. This burden lies upon the rich in so far as they control the lives of the poor by using up the earth's substance; and in this context, the rich include a majority of the people in the North, including the citizens of the Soviet Union.

There is of course no guarantee that the rich will pursue this particular course of self-interest. There are narrower, more familiar paths of self-interest which appear easier; and it may be that faith in the power of money extends to such a degree that they will prefer to believe that they can buy themselves a haven from planetary destruction, that they will be numbered amongst those for whom there will always be a seat 'on the last plane out of disaster'.

The green myth is calling people for the first time to take responsibility for the planet: it is no longer enough to go about your business dutifully, and to hope that Providence, or the powers that be, or even the hidden hand, will deal with the larger questions. It is asking for something which is, on the face of it, completely unreasonable. If people feel they cannot even influence or understand the events and processes that structure the life of their neighbourhood and street, how on earth can we dream of their taking responsibility for the affairs of the planet? The truth is that those local disaffections and bewilderments have their origin in the same global processes. The great emancipation comes from recognizing the connectedness between the daily round and the wheelings of the planets. The green myth demands more, but it also offers more – a vision and an enlightenment which dispel all the semi-voluntary ignorance, anxieties and fear in which our lives are passed.

14

Although the response of the West to the green myth is crucial, it would be wrong to imagine that its success depends entirely upon that response. The planet, after all, doesn't belong to the West, in spite of its long and continuing civilizing mission to the rest of the world. The likely reaction of Eastern Europe and of the Third World will have equally important consequences.

It might be felt that the Soviet Union, for instance, has an advantage over the West, in so far as its people have not been overwhelmed by the fruits of private consumption, and to that extent are less articulated to the remorseless dynamic of the market economy – although they are scarcely uninfluenced by the logic and necessities of an industrial society which they felt compelled to imitate in so many ways, with such violent and convulsive consequences. Further, there exists within the Communist tradition, however flawed it has been in practice, the idea that apparently autonomous economic processes can be shaped by human understanding and volition.

Of course, the slightest inflection in socialist practice is immediately hailed in the West as evidence that the Soviets have seen the error of their ways, and are being forced to defer to the superior mechanisms of the market economy. Thus, any movement the Soviets might make to renew their own socialist traditions by attempting to draw upon the green myth would inevitably be presented in the West as demonstrating the falsehood of socialism, and vindicating the Western way of life and its fundamentally truthful account of human nature. The reason why such a development would be difficult in the Soviet Union is the institutionalizing there of Marxism as an official myth, a Marxism which has as its very foundation the unquestioning belief that industrialism alone can free the forces of production.

Furthermore, this official myth has become so petrified and bureaucratized that the more supple and energetic modes of Western capitalism can be interpreted as a more successful alternative myth in the Soviet Union itself. The relative success of capitalism (at least in the rich countries) creates a powerful and seductive illusion that all the defective aspects of the Soviet system could be remedied by a judicious plundering of capitalist techniques (not to say technology). This renders them less susceptible to the green myth, unless they are prepared to trust the evidence of their own senses, by looking at what ruthless industrialization has done to their own country. Some indication of this was given by Boris Komarov, in his *The Destruction of Nature in the Soviet Union*, first published in the West (and only there) almost a decade ago:

The composition of the air, of our drinking and sea water is a state secret. These statistics are the property of the government, just like the earth, the rivers, and the forests and their denizens, the animals.

A Soviet citizen can get a fully detailed, disastrous picture of the state of nature in the United States or the Federal Republic of Germany. He can read in Russian agitated and profound books by Commoner, Parsons or Douglas. The poisoning of Lake Erie, the oil-drenched beaches of England, and the mountains of garbage in New York even flash before him on the TV screen to convince him of the advantages of his own socialist way of life ... The Soviet citizen must simply believe the statement that socialism itself, by its very essence, guarantees harmony between man and nature, that 'universal ownership of the means of production and of all the natural resources' foreordains the successful resolution of ecological problems in the USSR.

In early 1977, at one of the sessions of the USSR State Planning Committee, the record levels of lung cancer and other diseases of the respiratory tract in the Novokuznetsk and Kemerovo industrial regions were discussed. The first-born of socialist industry proved to be new smoky Manchesters and Pittsburghs. Was this an accident? ...

Contemporary Donetsk is renowned for the greenery on its streets and the cleanness of its air. The local botanical garden has raised dozens of splendid varieties of flowers and shrubbery resistant to environmental pollution. They brighten the area around many factories and mines.

But the statistics in the confidential reports lack floral borders: morbidity from lung cancer is 330 per cent higher than among the inhabitants of other cities. After this, don't the flowers on the broad municipal lawns seem like modest daisies over the graves? ... Shrubs and flowers cannot compensate for the high gas levels in many areas of the Ukraine ... planting industrial zones is not an easy matter, but it is often easier to alter the biological constitution of plants and force them to bloom in a smokestack than to change a bureaucratic system that defends nature mainly with resolutions on paper.

Komarov goes on to quote a speech given at the First Congress of Siberian writers in 1926:

'Let the fragile green breast of Siberia be dressed in the cement armour of cities, armed with the stone muzzles of factory chimneys, and girded with iron belts of railroads ... Let the taiga be burned and felled, let the steppes be trampled. Let this be, and so it will be inevitably. Only in cement and iron can the fraternal union of all peoples, the iron brotherhood of all mankind be forged.'

Komarov also points out that not only Communism, but the Christian world believed, without any sophistry, that God created man 'to exercise dominion over the fishes of the sea, and over the birds of the heavens and over the whole earth'.

The present reforming leadership of the Soviet Union has shown, however, a much deeper awareness of 'the global danger of an ecological "seizure"'. It may yet be that the countries of existing socialism, however unlikely their current pattern of development may make it appear, will turn afresh to the creation of that communism which Marx described in 1844 as a '*definitive* resolution of the antagonism between man and Nature, and between man and man'. If the requirements of a green Communism were to transcend the terms in which Marx made his own analysis, perhaps he would be less surprised, even less disappointed, than Marxists might imagine.

15

The fact that the consumer societies of the West appear to the people of the 'existing socialist' countries as a desirable alternative is founded on the same dualism which tethers the people of the West to the capitalism they know, by contrasting the benefits it provides with the disadvantages of 'existing socialism', which it declares to be the only – and deeply undesirable – alternative. The symbiotic polarization between East and West creates a powerful gravitational pull, the main ideological effect of which is to convey the conviction that these alternatives cannot be transcended. If you don't like one, you must choose the other. 'Get back to Russia' is no idle insult thrown at critics of the Western system: it is a fundamental closing down of any contestatory argument. Similarly, those who dissent from the Soviet system are represented at home as tools, willing or unwilling, of the capitalists, and in the West as aspirants to the only human freedoms which are available in this world. The green myth, because it offers a real transcendence of this stalemate, risks being outlawed by both – ironically, with the same contemptuous dismissal: 'Utopian' – not of either one of those 'real worlds', which are, given the material circumstances of earthly life, both constructs of the wildest imagination.

It might be thought that those Western countries which have experienced the furthest effects of the market economy are better placed to go beyond its disablements and inadequacies. If this appears not to be so (except possibly in the case of the Federal Republic of Germany), it is only partly on account of the disgracing of the socialist alternative as caricatured by the East in practice, and by the West in perception. Resistance to change is influenced even more by the fear of loss, by that dependency which capitalism generates in those who are its most refined products, its people. And yet, it is these very advanced developments within capitalism which acquaint people with its human costs, and with its limitless inroads to our deepest being. A consequence of this is that we are able to connect the inner depredations of capitalism with those outer ravages that are simultaneously taking their toll of both the people and their habitation, the world. It is this possibility of making connections that might dispose us to be more receptive of the green myth than the people of the Soviet Union. The apocryphal Gospel of Thomas instructs us that 'When you make the inner as the outer, and the outer as the inner . . . then shall you enter the Kingdom'; and although such celestial realms are not within the gift of politics, it must be observed that the creation of hell on earth most certainly is. The terror of their own emancipation is what holds the people of the West in chains. And as long as they see the only liberation on offer as a version of East European society, that terror does have a real basis in the world.

There are powerful reasons why the people of the South might be most open to accepting the message of green politics. They have been the victims of imperial processes which have regarded them as nothing more than the providers of raw material – the rawest of all being the people themselves – for industrial manufacture which has traditionally (though not always now) taken place elsewhere. They have seen the workings out of the logic of capitalism, in ways which the inhabitants of rich countries have been solicitously shielded from in recent years. They have seen the falling prices for the cash crops which were to have ensured their lasting prosperity, the installation of military regimes, the advisers of the IMF arriving in the capital, the subsequent rise in the price of bread or rice or transport, the riots on the streets and their bloody aftermath. If nevertheless they seem impervious to the hopeful resonance of the green myth, this is because they have seen their own traditional capacities for self-reliance, sufficiency and subsistence undermined, first by colonial invasion and later by forms of neo-colonialism that have integrated their countries disadvantageously into a single global economy. Against the disgracing of their own culture and practice and ways of living, the glamour and promise of Western wealth stands as a powerful inducement to leave the exhausted piece of ground and to make for the town or the city, which is the closest their country can offer to an imitation of the Western way of life. They are encouraged in this rejection of the local and familiar by the values and example of the elites in their own countries, who are surrogates of Washington or Moscow, both in their style of living and in the pattern of development they have imposed upon their people. Even for those growing numbers who see the worst effects of capitalist development, there always exists the possibility of choosing what appears to be its opposite – the Marxist myth. Nor does this by any means exhaust the possible alternatives that Third World peoples might choose before the green hope: the power of Islam, or indeed any other form of fundamentalism, carries opposition to both East and

West, and at the same time avoids any gesture of a green solution.

Against this, it is in the Third World that some of the most disastrous effects of the world economy appear in brutal and cataclysmic forms. When people see desert where they used to grow crops, when they see large landowners displace their labour with mechanized farming methods, when women must walk twenty kilometres a day for fuel or water before the people can eat, when the rainfall patterns are modified by the destruction of forests – which gave shelter and livelihood to whole peoples – then, whatever they may or may not know about the origins of these processes, they do know that a great sickness has fallen upon the places that sustain them. The rural poor, who after all still constitute a majority in the Third World, are the most vigorous potential allies in the propagation of green salvation. For them, green hope literally means survival; and that is the salvation upon which all others depend.

16

Although we are exploring the green myth as though it were new in the world, it does in fact draw upon themes and structures which are part of the mythic storehouse of humankind, and it shows particularly strong continuities with the founding stories of Western culture. At the root is the great Christian account of the order of things (itself a reworking of earlier elements of redemptive dramas). This is essentially a timeless epic of innocence ruined, and the hope of its restoration. It tells of paradise lost, and a long journey in the wilderness. It is both the sacred history of a people, and an archetypal narrative of the individual's journey through the world, expelled from paradise, wandering through pain and suffering. It is rich and resonant in the parallels between individual and collective effort. It tells also of the need for redemption, the necessity of sacrifice, if the richer life of eternity

From Christian Myth to Green Myth: A diagram

CHRISTIAN MYTH	EARLY CAPITALISM CAPITALIST MYTH: 1	LATE CAPITALISM CAPITALIST MYTH: 2	SOCIALIST MYTH	GREEN MYTH
1 Paradise: Garden of Eden	As Christian	Paradise is here and now	Classless society (primitive communism)	People in balance with nature
2 The Fall	Fallen Human Nature	Being cut off from money	Growth of private property	Seeking to dominate nature.
3 Wanderings: Years in the Wilderness	Individual striving	Search for money	History of class society up to development of capitalism	Industrialism
4 The redemptive Sacrifice	The work ethic	Sacrificing anything that gets in the way	Sufferings of the proletariat	Renunciation of a life that ruins the planet
5 The Resurrection	The soul saved and money gained	Spending	Development of class consciousness	Survival
6 The Day of Judgement	The passage to heaven earned	Every day is a day of judgement on what you can afford to buy	Day of revolution	Avoidance of apocalypse
7 Heavenly after-life *or* hell	As Christian – heaven or hell	Who cares?	Heaven on Earth *or* ruin of the contending classes	No heaven on earth *or* hell on earth

is to be won (paradise regained). This mythic drama is also to be played out in history, at the Day of Judgement, and it is to that moment that all earthly strivings must be articulated. After this final irruption of the eternal into time, the timelessness of heaven and hell is all that will remain.

This story has for a very long time furnished all the elements necessary to give meaning to human endeavour, both spiritual and material. Of course it has required modification, as social systems have gone through their mutations in time. It has been shown how the exigencies of economic development in the Middle Ages broke through the spiritual constraints upon human conduct, at both the social and individual levels. Of course people had constantly failed to live up to the spiritual standards set for them, but such failings were regarded as imperilling the immortal soul of the individual, before they were later transmuted into sound business eithics under the dominance of capitalism. As Tawney said, in *Religion and the Rise of Capitalism*: 'If it is proper to insist [in the Middle Ages] on the prevalence of avarice and greed in high places, it is not less important to observe that men called these vices by their right names, and had not learned to persuade themselves that greed was enterprise and avarice economy.' For most of its history, capitalism made extensive use of the Christian myth, using certain elements to compensate for its own rigours, and secularizing other aspects that stood in the way of its transformative project. Thus, while capitalist ideology clung on to the doctrine of the Fall, in order to justify the free play of greed, which was the best that could be expected from fallen human nature, it found it necessary to secularize the act of redemption into the work of accumulation. It thus established a happy congruence between those actions that would win both earthly and heavenly rewards.

This remains what we might call the 'Old Testament' of classical capitalism. It offers the new fundamentalists of our time

many profitable texts, however inappropriate such sermons may
be to the spirit which now animates capitalist realities in the late
twentieth century. So great has the divergence between classical
and contemporary capitalism become that we are almost compelled to postulate a 'New Testament', a revised version of the
capitalist myth. This new version represents a further secularizing
of the Christian myth. It no longer relies on borrowed sanctification from the Christian story, but on the contrary feels strong
enough to sacralize itself. Indeed, if once the chroniclers of
capitalism recorded how 'all that is solid melts into air, all that is
holy is profaned', we must now bear witness to the way in which all
the intangible qualities of human experience are forced to assume
material shape, while all the things of this world (and only the
things of this world) are made holy. In this version, which of
course has greater plausibility for the rich of the earth, eternity
and the present are indistinguishable. To be rich is to transcend;
to enjoy extreme wealth is to glimpse the beatific vision. Those
who describe this process as 'secularization' will be powerless to
struggle effectively against it.

They will also be powerless in so far as they cling to that myth
which came into the world precisely to vanquish and replace the
original myth which sustained capitalist development. For Marxism, too, shared the same root structure as that which sustained
classical capitalism and its Christian progenitor. Socialism was
also committed to secularization, but this did not prevent it from
depending upon the same sacred themes. Whilst denying any
need for religion, or indeed for myth of any kind, in its future
secular paradise, it nevertheless speaks, in altered terms, of a day
of judgement: the coming of the revolution which will lead to the
building of that earthly paradise, where we will move from the
realm of necessity into the realm of freedom – or more sombrely,
to the ruin of the contending classes, and a barbarism than which
no greater hell could be imagined. Nor is the state of primal

innocence neglected, as history moves from primitive communism, with its classless society and absence of private property, through a familiar story of the fall into private appropriation and class conflict, from which humanity is to be rescued by the redemptive struggles of the suffering working class.

To gain an adequate understanding of why socialism is now failing, we need to grasp the complexity of its relationship, at the level of myth, to contemporary capitalism. For in our time capitalism has radically reworked its own earlier transformation of the Christian myth. It has both expropriated the secularizing hopes of socialism, and conjured forth in new forms the wrappings and trappings of a religiosity which it had earlier outgrown. The socialist myth became dogma even while the capitalist myth, omnivorous and insatiable, sucked in an ever wider range of symbols, beliefs and fantasies to feed the raw energies that propel its own triumphal epic story.

It is from this context that the green myth derives its present power. In its intensely spiritual thrust, it refers back to the original Christian story, while its political urgency and concern for the things of this world make it the direct heir to the socialist endeavour. More than this, it has deep structural affinities with both the Christian and socialist myths. It too speaks of people originally living in a state of balance with nature (this is not necessarily to be understood as some kind of mystical harmony with nature, but rather as a clearsighted respect for the natural world which sustains all life, however hostile it may at times be), and of the fall, which is the doomed attempt to dominate nature, whereby nature becomes a mere source of raw material for industrialism. The wilderness in which we are in consequence condemned to wander is no metaphor: it is all too visible in the poisoned seas, the blighted landscapes, the barren fields around us. There is even the need for a redemptive sacrifice, for the green myth involves a radical transformation in the way we use the world, its people and its resources. This is not a sacrifice of our happiness or satisfactions, but rather the discovery of other forms of enjoyment and happiness than those which imperil our own survival.

There are, of course, significant divergences from the original Christian myth. The sacrifice is not going to be made by any suprahuman agency. There is no Redeemer, our salvation is in our own hands. It is a more modest salvation than that promised by Christianity, for the only immortality we are offered is that of the continued survival of our kind. Thus, while we may not look forward to a heaven on earth (or perhaps anywhere else), a kind of afterlife is nevertheless the reward; while the alternative is very clearly universal desolation, a version of hell upon earth.

The debt of the socialist myth to its Christian antecedent has already been made plain, and it is therefore not surprising that there are clear parallels between the socialist and green myths – including the fall from a version of 'primitive communism'. An important divergence comes in the role of industrialism in the two stories; but there is a similar sense of wandering through the wastelands of industrial society, and the same emphasis upon the centrality of the development of consciousness. Whereas the socialist myth relies upon the growing consciousness of one class, the green myth depends upon the self-realization of all humanity. Its true interests lie in a common endeavour. There is no redemptive class or agency to save the world (no Christ-figure, no proletariat, to do the work for us). This lack of an identifiable agent of transformation presents difficulties in both political analysis and action, although it has to be said that the traditional socialist and Christian theories both falter in the presence of a dying planet. The green myth does not, of course, foresee the end of time, or indeed the end of history; indeed, the avoidance of such endings of the human story is its most fundamental purpose in the world.

In spite of the differences, one of the most inspiriting and exciting aspects of the green myth is precisely its continuity with, and grounding in, the great informing beliefs of Western civilization (as well as those of many other cultures). It is these very affinities with both Christianity and socialism which tell us that the green myth is no arbitrary invention, no alien implant into the thought-patterns of either the West or the 'existing socialist' countries, or indeed of those traditional societies where respect for nature is still a central feature of daily experience and practice. The green myth grows from beliefs which have already demonstrated their power to transform both consciousness and the material world. But it offers more than a reconciliation of partly opposing traditions: it holds out the promise of fulfilling them, of taking both traditions one step forward into the future, of providing a new form in which their essential teachings can live on. It may even be that, looking back from a green future, we will regard with a certain tenderness the archaic contribution that capitalism made to the process that is unfolding. Capitalism may then be seen as a happy mistake, a 'felix culpa' without which our understanding of the oneness of the planet, and its deep interdependencies, would never have become possible.

People often ask 'But what would that green future look like?' – 'What would we do?' they want to know. 'How would it work?' – 'Describe the landscape, give us some concrete images.' It is extraordinarily difficult to respond to these demands. This is because we are living in a system which also lives through us, and inhabits us with such oppressive density that it fills our eyes and ears, all our senses, our imaginations and our minds, with the images, the fantasies, as well as the common sense, indeed the logic, of its own necessities. This leaves but little space for the imagining of alternatives, and when we seek to formulate these, they sound and appear banal in the presence of the vivid and violent and overwhelming imagery of capitalist actualities. How easy it is then for any such attempts to be dismissed as utopian, as impractical, as unrealistic, as naïve and doomed to failure.

And yet there are multitudes of people in Britain, as elsewhere in the world, whose lives are to some extent touched by diverse and interconnecting experiments in alternative ways of living. All the dissatisfactions with orthodox medicine, with its dependency upon chemicals and technology and its view of the human body as a spiritless machine, which have led to an intensifying search for other forms of healing; all those who have observed the invasion of the whole world by inappropriate technology and now practise more modest and resource-saving methods of growing, and making, and creating energy; the environmentalists braving the ridicule and violent repression of the authorities in Eastern Europe; the Chipko movement in India, whose supporters cling to the trees with their own bodies to prevent deforestation; the global movement to recuperate manufacture for local consumption, so that people in Manchester do not depend on green vegetables from Chile, so that people in the slums of Calcutta do not rely upon soap made by a secret formula held by American trans-national companies, so that the genetic structure of the crops grown in the fields of Thailand does not belong to companies whose headquarters are in Tokyo or Frankfurt – all these activities form part of a common project, which is the realization of the green myth in the world. They are not, as they are so often represented to be, lone and discrete gestures, but, on the contrary, are moved by the same informing hopes. When they all come together – the scientists resisting the mechanistic paradigms of their own tradition, and showing a new openness to the concerns of the spirit; all the professionals rejecting their own expertise, which they see as nothing more than wisdom expropriated from the people; those factory workers who are learning that their wages will never compensate for all that is taken out of them at work; the peasants seeing themselves displaced from their land by mechanized agriculture which denies them an income to buy enough food; the young people in the West beginning to pierce the veils that conceal connections between feasting at home and famine abroad; those who turn vegetarian because they see the slaughter of animals as yet another assault upon a suffering and impaired natural world, and, especially, because the crops used to feed animals could be feeding hungry human beings; women across the world making connections between the abuse of their labour and their sexuality, and the abuse of the earth that must bear us all – when all these come together, and the underlying sameness of our struggles is made known, both to ourselves and to the world, then the energies released and their transforming power in our lives will make us wonder why we ever doubted, and why we remained so long prisoners of our own fears.

17

However responsive people might be to the idea of the green myth, many will feel nevertheless that there is an insuperable objection to it: Human nature is simply not like that. Surely the system is so deeply entrenched in people's minds and consciousness that, whatever their aspirations, they cannot really change the way they live. They must still scramble for the last remaining parking space in the city centre, must stand at the checkout in Tesco's, have no choice but to scrape up a deposit for the mortgage, must continue to do work they have long ceased believing in, but of which they say apologetically (and for many, anachronistically) 'It pays the rent', or (even more archaically) 'It keeps the wolf from the door.' Others will simply object that it is asking too much of people.

Against that, there is so overwhelming a case to be made for the need for a radical break with the received wisdom and the customary way of doing things. Most people *do* want to survive, and *do* care about their children's future in a habitable world. More and more people may find it in their own interests to achieve what once they might have felt was impossible. It is also true that the terms on which capitalist versions of plenty have been offered have brought in their wake powerful dissatisfactions as well as much observable violence. Many people have a profound sense of disappointment. Is that all there is to it? Why the stresses, the anxiety, the exhaustion, the sense of futility if these really are the best arrangements that can be imagined?

We cannot, of course, claim always to know how other people make sense at an emotional level of the psychic violence and damage which the system inflicts. All we can do is indicate how these things have worked through us, and what solace is brought for us by the hopes borne by the green myth. Certainly it has the power for us to dissolve some of the feelings of helplessness, rage and impotence. This power may offer similar hope and energy to others. We cannot believe that, however idiosyncratic and specific our own histories may be, they do not share characteristics and feeling and responses with many others with whom we coexist in a common culture and experience. Indeed, the deeper we go into our own hearts, the more we find shared needs, fears, longings, all of them no doubt common to humanity, but which, in their particularities, are structured by the system which we inhabit, and which inhabits us.

JEREMY: During the period of working-class affluence, I always felt that something had gone obscurely wrong. It wasn't that I imagined for one moment that poverty was in any way desirable – given the history of my own family, it would have been both perverse and cruel to wish upon people any continuation of what had been their long-term experience. But any criticism of the forms of affluence to which people gained access in the 1950s and 1960s immediately brought forth scorn and incredulity: Why shouldn't people have the good things of life? Who are you to say it's wrong to aspire to what the rich have always enjoyed? There were accusations of puritanism, of resentment, of the defence of privilege, of elitism, of nostalgia for a mythic time when the working class was poor but happy, uncorrupted by materialism, or with its revolutionary consciousness (or its potential for it) relatively uncontaminated.

All of these were, I felt, unjust responses, although for many years I was unable to say exactly why. This earned for me the reputation of being immobilized by a backward-looking nostalgia. What troubled me was not that people's lives were better (who could be troubled by anything so clearly desirable), but what might be the consequences and longer-term effects of that particular form of improvement. Having observed the harsh and devitalizing poverty which the system had imposed upon the working class, it seemed strange, to say the least, that the system should now insist that they live with such heedless prodigality. The passage from one extreme to another was so abrupt. It was impossible not to wonder about a system anxious to brand all dissent as 'extremism', when that system itself oscillated so wildly. How could it be that frugality and self-denial could be a virtue for one generation and an unimaginable penance to the next? Why was it that comfort and ease could be promised at one moment to the people only after their death, while at another time, the search for comfort and ease was the purpose of this life, with no regard at all to any afterlife, or indeed to the life of the spirit at all? It was always difficult to believe that there was not a catch in it, that one day there would not be another price to pay beyond that at the point of purchase of all the good things suddenly available. Why did a system that seemed for generations to have resented and punished those it called into existence to serve it, now make those same people the object of such tender concern?

I didn't believe it. It was too good to be true; and too true to be really good. The doubts were neither idle nor simply personal. They were rooted in the place where I grew up, in the dissenting voices of the boot and shoe workers. Their scepticism, reserve, austerity, obstinacy, distrust of the pieties and orthodoxies of their time, their stinginess, their ability to remain unimpressed by wealth or power – these things were deeply rooted, and were, at the same time, both virtue and vice of that parochial, inward-looking but incorruptible sensibility. If it seemed moralistic and grudging to express reservations about the way that life was changing, I felt then that it must be the more damaging part of the dissenting inheritance that was speaking through me. Now, this no longer looks so clear.

Certainly, there was little enough confirmation of any such doubts either in political discourse or in the wider culture of the time. It was then that the Labour Party unequivocally gambled its own future – to say nothing of the future of the people it represented – on the continuation in perpetuity of the capitalist capacity for growth and expansion; and perpetuity is a long time. It seemed like an irrevocable commitment; and so it has proved.

Because the argument against what was happening was incompletely formulated, it was easily misrepresented; and such misrepresentation actually served to stifle debate. I became associated with a backward-looking nostalgia and pessimism, at a time when everybody knew that the future belonged to the Left and to those who still, at that time, purported to represent the working class. Thus, the way in which the transition from poverty to affluence occurred was shrouded in taboos and proscriptions. It was not until those forms of affluence which were once greeted as the ultimate liberation could be seen to involve a reappearance of the old evils – mass poverty and unemployment – that its nature and significance could begin once more to be discussed; and then only hesitantly and in part.

The green myth offers a way of making sense of the depth and extent of capitalist corruption in its present phase; for it illuminates the capacity, indeed the necessity of capitalism to *lay waste* not only the material but also the human resources which get squandered in its search for profit. Just as the world is full of derelict and abandoned mineworkings, polluted lakes, destroyed grasslands, the bleached boneyards of dead trees, poisoned watercourses and croplands returned to dust, so it is also littered with the casualties of the heroin and cocaine wars, alcoholics, the victims of both state and civil violence, the corpses of the under-nourished in a world of plenty, dispossessed subsistence farmers whose children have been turned into thieves and whores by slum existence, discarded factory and plantation workers, and the victims of the ever greater refinements of military technology. The passage of the peoples of the world from age-old poverty into a capitalist version of plenty entails a terrible and destructive cost. The transformation of the working class in the rich Western countries in the 1950s and 1960s changed them from the labour that had drawn the chariot of capital into the engines that propelled it with their desires. First by their labour, and then by their needs, the people remained harnessed to capitalist necessity. The violence this inflicted upon them, upon their fellow human beings, and upon the planet itself can only now be seen. What some tentatively felt to be vaguely wrong or undesirable then, now reveals itself to have been catastrophic, a major calamity. All those people who asked what was wrong with the working class – or indeed any other class – enjoying the fruits of industrial society can now see the answer inscribed on the face of the earth, and in the faces of countless millions of its inhabitants, not all of them the poorest. The chance for a decent sufficiency, a secure place in the world (which was all that an older working-class tradition had wanted) was bypassed and effectively suppressed, because the conditions on which capitalist improvements were to be made available required that the people remain subordinate to economic necessity, rather than that the economic system should be made to serve them. The green myth offers a possibility of liberation from these processes, both a recovery of more modest claims upon what the earth will bear, and a hope of surviving beyond tomorrow. It looks both backward and forward, and doesn't try to escape by hiding in a perpetual present which acknowledges neither its own roots, nor its own consequences.

Because the green myth is global, it makes the connections between the West and the poor parts of the world, connections which are collusively suppressed in Britain and elsewhere; shows how our 'privileges' are paid for by the poverty of others. Not only this, it illuminates processes which the British working class passed through some decades ago, and which other people all over the world are now being subjected to. Not only is the industrialization of the cities of the South a direct echo of British experience in the nineteenth century, but also peoples formerly self-reliant and living in balance with the natural environment are seeing that relationship degraded and broken by the necessities imposed by cash crops, agribusiness and deforestation. In India, the tribal peoples who knew all about survival in the forests are dispossessed of their practices and knowledge by the cutting down of the wood for industrial construction for the market. The dynamic of industrial society causes more and more people to pass directly or indirectly under its dominion, which means the loss of sustainable ways of living, the surrender of knowing how to survive without ruining the natural base. The project of liberation unites the people of both rich and poor parts of the world. The green myth offers hope, and it represents continuity with the more modest formulations of socialist endeavour. It speaks to us of a deindustrializing of our humanity.

TREVOR: I've always felt uncomfortable at political meetings, always distrusted 'political' people. Their certainties sounded so ill-founded, their slogans so inadequate, their righteousness so lacking in self-awareness. And yet, I've never been able to ignore politics either, because it is, in our time, the area in which moral arguments take place, the meanings of our lives in the world debated. Part of the importance of the green myth is that it reinstates the moral arguments back at the heart of politics.

Coming from a working-class Methodist background, I always had a strong sense of the need for social justice, for fairness in the world. I saw how the people I grew up with were often at the raw end of what, no doubt, seemed like necessary decisions to those who held power. On the other hand, I had a deeply religious childhood which left me with strong mystical inclinations and a fascination with the inner world.

During the 1960s I found the counter-culture a very exciting expression for this concern with the inner world, and I dealt with my vague feelings of guilt that I was living a very privileged life by the optimistic belief that we were moving into some post-scarcity society, where no one would need to work very much, and where we would all live like lords, or at least like spiritual aristrocrats. These contradictions were sharpened in Nepal, when I made 'the journey to the East' in the late 1960s. An image which seemed to crystallize it was going to visit two Tibetan lamas living on the top of a hill just outside Kathmandu. They lived in a large house loaned to them by the soothsayer of the King of Nepal. As I climbed the hill, it was impossible not to feel that a more than physical ascent was taking place. As the fields stretched out below, the figures working began to blend in with the landscape. It was at that point on the journey that I became uncomfortably aware of the contrast between my destiny and theirs. Work wasn't about to be abolished in the world, and the people bending over the crops were the kindred of those I had left behind in Blackburn. Furthermore, the spiritual ideologies in the East, which justified their humble position in the hierarchy of spiritual beings, had uncomfortable analogies with those doctrines in the West which taught that it was in the necessary order of things that the rich man should occupy his castle, and the poor man remain at his gate. I knew where this would have left my parents and myself a couple of generations ago. I felt unable to continue this pilgrimage which seemed either to banish social justice from its concerns, or, at best, to treat it as being of only minor importance compared with the great riches of the inner life.

This withdrawal seems to be a paradigm of how my whole life has been marked – by repeated oscillations between political and spiritual concerns, so that whenever I got involved in one, there has always come a point at which I retreated and swung over to the other. Neither the political nor the spiritual seemed to offer a satisfactory way of being. The green myth excites me, because it offers a possibility of bringing these two sets of concerns closer to each other, and perhaps even effecting a reconciliation. For although it is firmly grounded in pressing material concerns, and offers connections which explicate our own political life in Britain, it is also a deeply spiritual enterprise. It promises above all that we can still try to be good in the world, that we do not have to live in public by a set of alien values which we would never practise with those whom we hold dear. Behind it is a sense of the oneness of humanity, a sense of how we can learn to be *kind* in the old meaning of the word.

Recently I went down to Wales to spend the weekend at the Alternative Technology Centre. Saturday was a beautifully sunny day, and we went for a walk above the slate quarry and across the fields. As we reached a high point, we suddenly saw the Dovey valley down below us. Through the valley a silver river wound down to the sea, and on either side green fields spread out to the mountains and the hills. In between the mountains were layers of mist, so that they looked like cardboard cut-outs. And in the far distance the sun shone over the water. It looked like paradise

– paradise regained. For a moment it was difficult to imagine how anyone could be unhappy living in such a world. And I felt we'd been given a second chance.

A second chance to redeem in the 1980s and 1990s the faded hopes of the 1960s. The 1960s were a very important cultural moment, and, in spite of all their excesses and naïveties and self-indulgence, they carried some of the seeds of our present hopes.

The Green movement should not deny its links with the much-derided hippies. Yes, the hippies were silly; yes, they took too many drugs; yes, they confused desiring and achieving; yes, they failed to throw off the hierarchical values of the straight society they claimed to despise; yes, for some it was just a matter of middle-class kids dressing up and smoking dope. Nevertheless, the hippies helped to release the energies on which all significant radical political movements ever since have fed.

Of course we need to go beyond those rudimentary alternatives, but, when the 1960s are constantly vilified by populist-authoritarian Conservatives as being the source of all permissiveness, of the breakdown of the family, of sexual promiscuity, of the collapse of the work ethic, of being, indeed, the source of all our present evils, it is important to defend the 1960s, and to acknowledge that inheritance as one important source of the greening of our thinking.

The green myth offers the hope that what was dissolved in the pipe-dreams of the 1960s can be articulated and worked for at a much deeper level in the closing years of the twentieth century. This time round we are a little wiser, a little more experienced, and we have suffered more. Where we went wrong, where our understanding was inadequate, we have paid the price in our own lives, and some of our friends have paid it with their deaths. But we do not have to live as those without hope in the world. Green politics offers a matrix for our hopefulness.

18

Some years ago in his book on *Marxism and Christianity*, Alasdair MacIntyre argued that in the end he remained a Marxist because 'the Marxist project remains the only one we have for re-establishing hope as a social virtue'. In our time, it is the green philosophy which makes social hope possible; and amidst the impotence and frustration and dividedness that contemporary capitalism inflicts, this hope is essential and necessary if we are not to retreat into what are sometimes described – perhaps falsely – as our private lives.

The green myth carries forward the very essence of the socialist project, but places it in the context of what is sometimes called late capitalism – a capitalism which threatens to become too late for our survival. To many people, this concern for myths might seem of marginal importance to the stuff of politics. This is not so, for all politics revolves around the telling and retelling of a few stories. The green story is still in the process of being told; it hasn't, as yet, got a final version or a classical form; there is still room for all kinds of improvisation and elaboration.

Sooner or late the myth must pass into politics. It has to be lived out in the world through us. Thus it is that the story becomes history. Such stories are not abstractions. They must be acted out by flesh and blood. And yet, when they do take root in people's lives, they tend to harden and become revelation, demanding that human creatures adapt themselves to that known inner structure. It is then that the myths become damaging and destructive, like the capitalist or Marxist myths; or they become simply irrelevant, like dissenting sects stranded by toleration.

The most difficult thing is to know when a story has outlived its usefulness, for we do not only live by stories; they also live through us. This is what makes the story of Labourism and the myth of its power to humanize capitalism so poignant. Its story has become part of our internal development, and we still want to see the world through its familiar prism. After all, did it not give light to those who brought us into the world, and to their parents before them?

To renounce our childhood stories requires a real sacrifice, indeed a betrayal. Yet without a certain kind of betrayal, growth is not possible. Many myths indicate the necessity of passing through three stages of development: the moment of withdrawal from life as we have lived it; the moment of transition (which is also a kind of death); and the moment of return or rebirth, bearing a gift from the underworld. These stories also tell us that if this deepening self-awareness is not chosen, it must then be endured.

Because of the way we have used the world in the past two centuries, we have reached a moment when the fate of both the inner and outer worlds have become closer than ever before. This gives a compelling urgency to our attempts to work through the impasse of socialist politics in the 1980s. For if we do not read the signs of the times aright, the day will also come when we can no longer discern the face of the sky.

NOTES

I

We have also explored the history of the period from the 1940s to the 1980s in our previous book, *A World Still to Win* (Faber, 1985), where we argue that far from having 'disappeared' or become middle class, the working class has undergone a profound reconstruction in accordance with the modified imperatives of the new global division of labour. This now links more inescapably than ever before the destinies of the car workers of Cowley, the low-paid service workers up and down the country, and the school-leavers on the Youth Training Schemes, with the fate of the garment workers in the sweatshops of Bombay, the coffee workers on the plantations of Brazil, and the electronic assembly workers in the factories of Seoul and Taipei. This world-embracing extension has entailed an ever-deeper penetration, and more violent reworking of the very psychic structures of working people, as capitalism has learned that no less spectacular profits are to be made from its exploitation of the heart and the spirit and the imagination, than may be won from the flesh and blood of those who live under its dominion. These developments have immediate and unavoidable implications for all those who would link radical changes with the evolution of working-class consciousness.

The general conclusion we draw is that the story of the post-war working class has been the history of a remaking, whereby the working class have appeared only as beneficiaries of capitalism's particular version of material progress, and not as victims of a violent restructuring of the psyche and emotions, which has been undertaken in such a way that the needs of the people have remained subordinate to the more pressing needs of autonomous economic process. The transformation thus worked has brought to an end one set of possibilities for radical change, borne within a tradition of labourism. This moment is irretrievable, and as a result, the elaboration of a new politics becomes at the same time more difficult and more imperative. In the light of this historic failure, the emancipation of humankind can no longer wait upon the destiny of the proletariat: even though, if we are not to suffer similar disillusionments in the future, we can neither abandon the working class, nor attend upon any other single agent of transformation to show us the way.

2

There are, of course, many different working-class responses to being gay. A more tolerant and generous attitude is portrayed in Tom Wake-field's *Forties' Child*, Routledge and Kegan Paul, 1980, and *Mates*, Gay Men's Press, 1983.

5

For further interpretations of gay politics and lifestyle in the 1970s, see Gay Left Collective, *Homosexuality, Power and Politics*, Allison and Busby, 1980; Jeffrey Weeks, *Coming Out*, Quartet, 1977, and *Sexuality and its Discontents*, RKP, 1985; and Jeremy Seabrook, *A Lasting Relationship*, Allen Lane, 1976.

An example of how socialists have sometimes too uncritically conceded the progressive nature of capitalist development is Marx's and Engels' song of praise to capitalism and the bourgeoisie in Section 1 of the *Manifesto of the Communist Party*:

'The bourgeoisie, during its rule of scarce one hundred years, has created more massive and more colossal productive forces than have all preceding generations together. Subjection of Nature's forces to man, machinery, application of chemistry to industry and agriculture, steam-navigation, railway, electric telegraphs, clearing of whole continents for cultivation, canalization of rivers, whole populations conjured out of the ground – what earlier century had even a presentiment that such productive forces slumbered in the lap of social labour?'

PART TWO: FAITHS

8

There is a useful collection of Marx's writings on religion in K. Marx and F. Engels, *On Religion*, Foreign Languages Publishing House, Moscow, 1955. For some of the connections between Marxism and religion see

Alasdair MacIntyre, *Marxism and Christianity*, Pelican, 1971, and Trevor Ling, *Karl Marx and Religion*, Macmillan, 1980.

R.H. Tawney's classic study *Religion and the Rise of Capitalism* was first published in 1926, and is currently available in Penguin.

9

On the connections between our eating habits and other people's hunger see: Francis Lappé and Joseph Collins, *Food First*, Sphere, 1982; Susan George, *How the Other Half Dies*, Penguin, 1976; and Teresa Hayter, *The Creation of World Poverty*, Pluto, 1981.

10

For sociological discussion of the meaning of religion in modern society see: R. Bocock and K. Thompson, eds., *Religion and Ideology*, Manchester University Press, 1985; Thomas Luckman, *The Invisible Religion*, Macmillan, 1967; and Peter L. Berger, *The Capitalist Revolution*, Wildwood House, 1987.

11

The description of the Victoria Centre in Nottingham, is taken from J. Seabrook, *What Went Wrong*, Gollancz, 1978.

12

The description of the Indian Mutiny comes from Christopher Hibbert, *The Great Mutiny: India, 1857*, Penguin, 1980.

PART THREE: FUTURES

13

On the power and meaning of myth see: C.G. Jung, *Memories, Dreams, Reflections*, Fontana, 1977, and *Man and his Symbols*, Aldus Books, 1979; Joseph Campbell, *The Masks of God*, Penguin, 1987; and *Myths to Live By*, Paladin, 1985.

The Bahro quotation is taken from 'Towards a general theory of the historic compromise' in *Socialism and Survival*, Heretic Books, 1982.

15

For the connections between the countries of the Third World and the 'advanced' industrial societies, see: Peter Worsley, *The Three Worlds*,

Weidenfeld and Nicolson, 1984; Michael Redclift, *Development and the Environmental Crisis*, Methuen, 1984; Paul Ekins, ed., *The Living Economy*, RKP, 1986.

16

There is a rapidly growing literature on all aspects of green politics. The following are particularly useful: Jonathon Porritt, *Seeing Green*, Blackwell, 1984; Walter and Dorothy Schwarz, *Breaking Through*, Green Books, 1987; Charlene Spretnak and Fritjof Capra, *Green Politics*, Paladin, 1985; Rudoph Bahro, *Socialism and Survival*, Heretic Books, 1982, and *From Red to Green*, Verso, 1984; André Gorz, *Ecology as Politics*, Pluto, 1983; James Lovelock, *Gaia: A New Look at Life on Earth*, OUP, 1979; Peter Russell, *The Awakening Earth*, RKP, 1982.